LUCAS

THE MANNING DRAGONS BOOK 4

KATHI S. BARTON

World Castle Publishing, LLC
Pensacola, Florida
Copyright © Kathi S. Barton 2018
Paperback ISBN: 9781629899879
eBook ISBN: 9781629899886
First Edition World Castle Publishing, LLC, September 3, 2018
http://www.worldcastlepublishing.com

Cover: Karen Fuller
Editor: Maxine Bringenberg

Chapter 1

Lucas hated to be in the hospital. Actually, he hated any place where he was inside. He preferred the outdoors, even when it was cold or raining. It was where he felt the most alive. When someone knocked on the door, he gently turned his head to it. Since being shot, Lucas about puked every time he moved too quickly.

"How you feeling?" He told Cooper that he was feeling pretty good except for the dizziness. "Yes, I would imagine that would be something that you'd have. You were shot. Did they tell you that?"

"No. No one mentioned me taking a bullet and it took me a while to figure out. I'm guessing the reason that I'm still here is because it was either iron or steel. Where is my doctor? I think she's avoiding me." Lucas frowned at his older brother. "I'm embarrassed at the things I said to her. When she came in here this morning, I realized my mistake. But she did smell great."

"Yes, she had a talk with all of us, asking us if you ever had this sort of issue before." Lucas asked if she really called it an issue. "Yes. She knows all about us, as you can imagine with her being a doctor and all. But the fact that you claimed she was something else to you sort of set her off into the world of unknowing. Not mad, but she had thought that the bullet might have done more damage to you than she'd first thought."

He could see that. When the door opened again, Lucas started to tell the good doctor that he was sorry once more when she simply lifted her hand up. Cooper laughed and stood up. Lucas asked him to stay and he declined.

"I have baby duty later—I still have a lot of things to get done while she's with her mother." He turned to the doctor and put out his hand. "Thank you so much for taking such good of my little brother."

"You're very welcome." Doctor Carver sat down beside the bed when Cooper left. Her smile, for some reason, was not very reassuring. "I wanted to tell you straight up that you should be dead. The bullet had pierced your heart. If it hadn't been for your sister-in-law telling me about you being an immortal, I would never have believed it."

"Lucky for me that was a power given to me just the day before." She nodded. "I'm truly sorry for saying those things to you. I think, as you asked me once, I hit my head a little harder than I thought. You also told me that the man and the bank manager are both dead."

"Yes. Someone here was treating him for his mental problems and had been for some time. They adjusted his meds for some reason, and we're believing that is what had him going to the bank." Lucas nodded. "The entire county and beyond think that you nearly died. As you've more than likely done in the past, we have to play it up for the cameras and the others out there. I would suggest a couple of more days. In fact, I'd like to insist on it. I know that you're still having trouble with the dizziness, correct?"

6

"Yes. It makes me ill to move too quickly." Doctor Carver asked him if he was still sick after he stood up. "Just a little. Not as much as when I move my head. I can walk well, just the quick movements."

"I've done an MRI on you and had someone come in and have a look, as you know. I'm thinking that it's a pulled muscle or a pinched nerve. There is no other explanation that I can find to tell us why that is going on." He nodded, saying he supposed a neck sprain was possible. "I've talked to your family, and they told me that you'd been under a little stress lately."

"Yes. I'm helping the family out with some investments. As well as a few other projects that I have a hand in. It's very time consuming, but I like it." He looked around the room slowly and noticed that there were more flowers than had been there yesterday. "I've been an attorney a few times in my lives, and it's served us when it was needed."

"Your brothers also told me that you've bought several buildings downtown, help the kids at their garden plots when you have time, as well as being involved in four more 'projects.' You're not going to get any better if you don't slow down. Do you have anyone working for you?" He told her his helper was on vacation. "Alan Peck?"

"Yes. How did you know?" Doctor Carver told him that Alan had been in to see him, and one of the others told her how Alan had been on vacation. "He didn't come home for me, did he?"

"I wouldn't know." She stood up. "Mr. Manning, you have family. I would like to suggest that you start having them or someone help you out. You're stressed, and you need to calm down. Having immortality would be horrific if you couldn't enjoy it."

After she left him, he lay there on the bed thinking. He could have gone home, she told him, but he decided to do what she said and stay on a few more days. Also, he was scheduled to have a cat scan soon, and that might tell them what was going on. Closing his eyes, Lucas tried to relax his body.

How about I tell you a bedtime story? I can even modify it so that there is blood and guts in it if you wish. He smiled when he realized that Carson had spoken to him. *The doctor just called Cooper and told him what she thinks and wants you to do. If I were you, I'd jump on that so that you tell Cooper what your plans are before he gets to order you to listen to the doctor. It'll make my day.*

He did just that and could hear the frustration in his voice when he told Cooper he was going to stay at the hospital for some extra time and would try his best to delegate more when he was working. Lucas was still laughing when he told Carson what he'd done.

He's none too happy with me at the moment. She told him congratulations on upsetting Cooper's plans to make him do it. *You sound a little sad. What's up? Anything I can help you with?*

That is the very reason you're stressed, you know. He told her that loving her wasn't stressful. *Yeah, sure it's not. No, I don't have anything going on that you could help me with. Unless, of course, you're lactating and would come and help me feed my baby.*

No. No thanks. I don't think I'd enjoy that all that much. But seriously, what is it? She didn't answer him, and he tried again. *I might not be able to help you, love, but I know a great many people that would jump at the opportunity to do something for me. Just say the word.*

I'm bored. I love being a mom, especially when the boys came here. They're like a breath of fresh air in my day. But I'm not able to be gone for long because I have to feed the little one, and even when Cooper is here, he's not really. I mean, I love him to death, but he's not much in the way of conversation when he comes home and shuts himself up in the office. He asked her why she'd not told him that. *I don't know. I guess because I figured that if the door was closed, not to come in. Not bother him.*

Nah, he's just closing the door because he's done that all his life. He might leave it open once in a while, but he'll eventually get up to shut it. I'm sure that it still stems from being hunted for so long. You have to remember that Cooper was the oldest of us, and saw how the humans treated our kind a lot more than any of us. She said she'd not thought of that. *I'm sure that if you asked him, he'd say he didn't even realize he was doing it.*

I thought for sure that he was telling me to stay out of his domain. Lucas said that Cooper would never do that to her. *I think that you're right on that. I'll work on that for myself. So, you didn't find your mate. I have to tell you, you were funny right after you were shot. I've never seen someone so hell bent on leather as you were to have a mate. I'm just glad that the doctor wasn't her, by the way. She has three children and a husband that worships her. But she's out there, Lucas. Don't give up because of this. I want to see you happy — all my new brothers happy, as a matter of fact.*

I won't. I promise. This was just a bump in the road, I guess. He looked around the room. *I have a favor to ask of you. There are a lot of flowers in vases in my room. I'm going to be here for a few more days. Do you think you could arrange for them to be picked up and put out for the little creatures before they're no longer good for them?* Carson said she thought that was a wonderful idea. *You remember that, so you can tell my actual mate what a guy I am.*

She was still laughing when the connection was broken. He, like his brothers, loved Carson—hell, all the women in the family. They had taken his brothers to a level of kindness that he'd never seen before. Not that they'd not been kind before, but now they were more accepting of change and showing their affections.

9

When his supper was brought to him, he was surprised to see the bag it was in was from one of his favorite all time restaurants. Opening it up, he read the note before digging into the food.

Hey. Knew you had to be sick of the food there, so I thought of you when I was at Submarines this afternoon. If I can, I'll have the rest of the guys bring you something better for each meal. Love you, little bro, Hudson.

Opening the foil around the first of two subs, he was so happy to find that it was also his favorite — meatball. He could literally eat them for every meal. Biting into the crisp bread with the soft inside, he moaned when he also tasted the sauce and meatballs. If he kept getting food like this to be delivered, he might survive staying in the hospital. Not really, but it would make it slightly more tolerable.

Lucas ate both subs and the large bag of cookies that were in the bag. He usually didn't eat sweets that much — they were something that he really enjoyed but kept himself from eating. Now that he knew that he needed to be less stressed, he decided to enjoy food a little more. In moderation, he told himself. There wasn't any point in over indulging too much — he'd burn out. Lucas lay back. Things were going to be better for him soon.

~*~

Micky ran each item over the scanner as the two women in her line spoke. Well, argued. The woman in line behind the person she was checking out was screaming at the first woman. Something about food cards and eating things like frozen pizza and other convenience foods. Micky didn't care so long as no one killed anyone.

Murdering someone had become the way people dealt with things that they didn't like. If someone were to argue with someone, or even have a driver cut them off on the highway, the solution was to pull out a gun and kill them. It was one of the reasons that she didn't drive. Another reason was that she didn't own a car. Not that she couldn't afford one, she told herself as the produce was weighed and bagged; she could. But that would mean dipping into her savings account, or any number of places that she had money stashed, and she wasn't going to do that.

Just as she was finishing up the groceries, the second woman totally lost her shit when the total for the first woman came to over two hundred dollars.

"Why are you able to spend that much on groceries when I can barely afford to feed myself on what I make?" The woman she was helping didn't engage but handed Micky the card that would pay for her food. "You have to answer me. I'm the one making it so you can have food on your fucking table, by God. I work my ass off so that you can laze around your house, eating whatever you can microwave or pop in a toaster, as your—"

"You think I like being on this card? You think that I'm sucking on the tit of society? Well I have news for you. If it were to bring my husband back to me, I'd surely give up being able to feed his four children and myself. He died for you and your freedom to have free speech. Well, right now, you can go and fuck yourself and your freedom of speech. I'm a mother of four small children that have no idea why their father isn't coming home to us. I was suddenly thrust into being the head of a household that I'm barely holding on to, if you fucking care. And since going back to work just after giving birth to his fourth child, his little boy, his sisters and I are needing some help." She looked at Micky with tears in her eyes and on her cheeks. For the first time since working here, Micky wanted to hug someone. "I'm sorry, but you'll have to help me trim this down. I didn't realize that I'd gone over."

She'd gone over by twelve dollars. When Micky started to tell her she'd cover it, the man behind the two women spoke up. He told her that he'd get it, that it would be his pleasure. Everyone in the store had heard the exchange, she realized, when a few more people decided to help her out too.

After Milly—that was her name—thanked them all, especially the first man, for helping her, she went to her car. But while she was loading up, the man, finally getting his turn to check out, asked Micky to hurry, as he wanted to give his cart load of food to Milly as well. Fourteen men and woman also donated, not just groceries, but cash. One woman bought her a gift card, telling her that she might have bills that it would take care of.

Micky was walking home that night when she thought of the woman. She wondered if it was a scam. She'd heard it had happened before. Not where she worked, but another grocery store. The person would stand in line and wait to be abused. Then when the shit hit the fan, so to speak, they'd have this sob story all thought out, so they could get not just food, but cash as well. Micky smiled. She needed to think of better things than scams.

There wasn't any trust in her either, not for human kind. She was human herself and she knew a great many shifters, but she didn't trust. Anyone. She hadn't always been like she was now. Micky had learned the hard way not to even trust family.

She had two sisters and a mother that were around, but she never engaged with them, nor did she try and seek them out when she had time to visit. They weren't people that she trusted either, especially her mom. Mariam Mantle was as shifty as anyone she knew. So were her sisters; Me-Me—her nickname that she'd given herself—and Bethany.

Me-Me's actual name was Mariam too. Giving herself

such a cutesy nickname was something that she had done to differentiate herself from their mom. Bethany hadn't stood for any nickname. It had always been Bethany, which she supposed was the reason that Micky called her Beth. And Me-Me, she was called Mariam the Second. It was the small things that got her through.

Micky's apartment was small, but she loved it. It wasn't in the best of neighborhoods, but it wasn't that bad either. She could come and go as she pleased, and there was a front doorman, the landlord's son, who wasn't there more often than he was. Micky was glad for that too, since every time she saw him he bugged her to go out with him. There wasn't any way that she'd go out with Sam Adams for all the money in the world. He was a jerk.

Putting her smock up, she sat her purse on the table. She would have a sandwich and then sit on the couch until it was time for her to go to bed. Yes, she thought, you do have a sorry life lately. Micky thought of her life thus far.

She had been engaged once. The man that she had fallen in love with had hung himself rather than spending the rest of his life with her. It had devastated her so badly that she had cut herself off from everyone and everything for a long time. Actually, she sometimes still had trouble with people.

Micky turned on the light on to read a bit. At just after seven, someone knocked on her door. If it was someone begging for money for some campaign, or even Sam, she was going to go straight to the landlord and complain. This was just annoying. Opening the door, the man she saw standing there looked confused for several seconds before he spoke.

"Mariam Mantle?" She said that she was Micky. And like everyone over the age of ten, he asked about her name. "Are you really Micky Mantle?"

13

"So it says on my birth certificate. Mariam is my mother or sister; depends, I guess, on what the birthdate is." He told her. "My mother then. She doesn't live here. Never has, as a matter of fact. You have the wrong Mantle."

"I'm to serve her." Micky told him that she couldn't help him with that either. "You have no idea where your mother might be?"

"Not if I can help it. And if I did know, I'd tell you. Someone needs to put her behind bars." He asked her if she wanted to know what she was being served for. "Nope. Whatever she's done, not paid for, or stolen, I had nothing to do with it. The only time I see her is when she's breezing through town and needs a place to flop. Not that I allow that, but she tries."

"You don't like her." She said nothing, but he seemed to understand. "All right, Miss Mantle. I'll try elsewhere for her. Thanks for your time."

Shutting the door, her phone started to ring. Micky thought that she was about the only person in the entire state with an actual phone. She didn't have a cell phone, cable, or even a computer. But she had a phone that hung on the wall. Smiling, she answered it.

"What do you have to say for yourself?" Mariam the Second, her voice as shrill and nasal as it could have been. "I asked you a question, Micky, and I expect an answer."

"You asked me what I had to say for myself. Since I haven't any idea what this could be about, just tell me so that I can either tell you to go to hell or to fuck off. It doesn't matter to me." She heard Mariam's sharp intake of breath and knew that she was going to scream at her about something. "When you call the next time, make sure that you explain yourself better than you did this time."

Hanging up the phone felt good. She knew that it would

14

be short lived, this feeling. It would piss off her sister to the point of her making a real nuisance of herself. So, when it rang again, she took her time answering it, waiting until the machine kicked in to take her message. Instead of answering it, like she'd planned, she let Mariam the Second rant.

"You fucking bitch. Wait until I tell Mother what you've done this time. You are going to be in so much trouble." Micky wondered if her sister realized that she was nearly twenty-five and had stopped caring what her mother had to say about her personal life when she'd been a teenager. "You need to bail out Bethany. I don't know what they're accusing her of, but she's always been the nice one. You never have. She's at county —"

Micky was glad that there had been a timer on her machine. That way Mariam the Second had to call back. And she did so, three more times. The entire exchange could have just taken the one message, but Mariam the Second had to pull out all the stops and call her every name in the book. It might have been funny if it wasn't so pathetic of her sister.

When she called back the sixth time, Micky answered the phone. Mariam was on a roll now and cursed at her again. Hanging up on her without saying a word, she waited until it rang once more before picking it up again. Mariam was much calmer this time.

"I want you to go to county lock up and pay to have Bethany gotten out of jail. This is all your fault anyway." Micky asked her how that was possible. "You didn't let her come and stay with you when she left her husband. The jerk was curtailing her spending. Like he didn't have the money to burn."

"I didn't even know Beth was married." Mariam corrected her on the name and said that she'd been married last year. "Last year? Well, I guess by now she'd have it down pat on divorcing husbands. What one is this one? Four? Five?"

"Seven. And what do you care for? It's not like you send out Christmas cards or birthday cards. You've never sent one to my children, much less me." Micky said that she didn't care for her or her children. "What a horrible thing to say. My children are my life."

"I'm sure that they are. And someday they're going to get life in prison for the way they act like rules don't apply to them." Mariam told her that they were exploring the world and that wasn't a crime. "No, I don't suppose you'd think so. But armed robbery and selling drugs, to most people anyway, is a crime. I guess you have your own set of rules, just like Mom and Beth do."

"It's Bethany. And why shouldn't we? We pay our taxes. We aren't on welfare like most people that you more than likely hang with. Why shouldn't we have a set of our own standards as to how we live?" Micky just laughed. "When can I tell Bethany you're coming? She's been in holding all day, and she wants to go home."

"I'm not sure what you think I'm going to do, but I'm not paying to have her bailed out. You do it." Mariam told her that her husband had put her on a budget, which didn't include bailing her sister out. "I always knew that Michael was a smart man."

"I've not been married to Michael for nearly ten years. You should be ashamed of yourself for not knowing that. But my new husband, Neil Patterson, is a great deal smarter than I thought he was. I will be filing for divorce from him soon enough. I just have to stash away more money first." Micky decided to find out who he was and let him know what his wife was doing. "Now that we've established that I'm not able to do it, that only leaves you."

"No, it doesn't. And no, I'm not doing it. You'll have

16

to figure something else out. What did they arrest her on, anyway?" She told her. "Making a nuisance of herself? Yeah, well that does sound like something that Beth would do. Who did she bother? I'm sure that it was someone she wanted to accuse of something."

"It's Bethany, which isn't that hard of a name to remember, Micky. Say it with me. Bethany. And she had every right to be there at her former home. She hadn't been able to get her things out of the house before he had the locks changed. What a horrible man to do that to our sister."

"She's only my sister when she or you want something. Same with you. I'm not going to do it. And don't call here again. I won't be answering the phone when you call."

Hanging up this time felt better than it had before. Taking the phone off the hook so that it would ring busy, she went back to her book and decided to just go to bed. Her family always landed on their feet, and this time, Micky knew, would be no different.

Going to bed, Micky knew that she wasn't going to rest well. Whenever she had to deal with her family it was the same thing. She'd be all stressed out and her belly would rebel. Micky tried to count sheep and then name the presidents and their vice presidents. When neither worked, she got up to go to work. Today was going to be hard, she knew that. One or all of them would be looking for her.

Micky decided at the last minute to leave her purse at home with her cards and money in it. All she had on her when she left was her lunch, having left her keys inside as well. There was a hidey key that she could get in with, so she felt like she was safe from them taking what didn't belong to them. She told her boss about them as she clocked in. He said that he'd be ready for them. She hoped she was too.

Chapter 2

Lucas counted to ten three times before he thought it was safe for him to speak. Carson had been at his home when he arrived with a list of things he was going to do for himself. One of them was that he was going to go flying with his brothers more. And actively look for his mate.

"I can tell when you're pissed, Lucas. This is something that you have to stop doing as well—not telling someone off when they make you mad." He just glared at her. "That is not telling me off."

"No, and I won't, either. Because I know for a fact that if I tried that you'd tell Cooper, or he'd just find out and I'd be back in the hospital with several more broken bones, as well as a large amount of blood loss." She snickered at him. "Carson, go away. I'm learning how to do this, but you harping on me endlessly is making me more stressed than before. Please? I'm begging you, just go home."

She left him with the list and several phone numbers. If he couldn't find his mate, then he needed to get laid. He threw them both in the trash. Sitting in the living room, he closed his eyes and thought of all the things Doctor Carver had told him. He was going to go by her list, not everyone else's.

He needed to eat better—not just better food but eating period. Sometimes when he was working, he'd forget to have a meal or two. That wasn't helping him either. A hungry dragon was a stressed one. She also told him to get out more.

"You mean get laid." She said that wasn't what she meant, but that wouldn't hurt him. "I don't know a lot of women. I mean, I know a great many, but none that I'd want to have casual sex with."

"I can understand that. I was talking to a friend of mine, a witch. But, and this is what you need to hear, she said that even if you were a true immortal, you could still have a heart attack, as well as any kind of ailment that could affect your mind. You need to relax that part of you as well." He said that he'd try. "No, Lucas, you have to do this. If your mate is out there, she's not going to be happy with having to take care of you because you had an aneurysm burst in your head. I don't know for sure if that could happen to you, but why take the chance?"

He didn't know either, but she was right. Why take the chance? So today, when he'd gotten home, he made a list of the projects that he had to deal with and a couple of other things. When it became overwhelming for a moment, he'd just lay the paperwork down and take several deep breaths. On one of those occasions, Alan came into the room with him.

"I have a list of people that can help you out. I've been telling you for years you needed help. I'm sorry that you had to go through this to get some, but I'm also glad. Here you go." Lucas took the list and looked it over. "I've put an assignment by each of the names that you're working on. I've taken care that they're all bonded, as well as had an extensive background check done on them."

"You've been busy since you came home." Alan told him that he might not the next time he got hurt while he was away. "I'm truly sorry for that. You shouldn't have come here. I was just fine."

"Yes, I'm sure that you think so. But I'm back and things are going to change. All right?" Lucas nodded. "Great. Now, as I was saying, I've hired four more people to your payroll. They are all very good at what they do, and you're going to use them."

"What is it that they're going to be doing for me? I'm not dead—I can do some things." Alan sat down in the chair across from him. He could see what him being hurt had done to the man. "I'm going to do what the doctor tells me, and if you can get me more help, then that's what I'm going to do. Just don't treat me as a fragile egg. I think that would stress me out more than all of this did."

"All right. But you will have to make changes, Lucas. You're a dragon who rarely gets away from the desk. You need to be you more." Lucas agreed with him. "Thank you. You read over the names I gave you, and I'm going to have one of the men that you hired go through the buildings and tell us what is needed to bring them up to code."

Lucas approved all the updates on the buildings—there were quite a few of them, too. Mostly they were abandoned at the moment. Lucas figured that he'd sell a couple of them and rework the others. By lunch time he was finished and gave Alan all the paperwork.

"I'm going to go get me some lunch. If you don't have plans." Alan said that he didn't, but he'd turn on the machine and go out too. "Good. We'll have to set something up to catch calls for us other than that machine. You know how much I hate that thing."

"Yes. I figured that out when I came back and there were fifty-seven messages on it." Alan laughed with him and said that he'd be back in an hour. Lucas said the same thing and headed to the elevator.

Going to the main lobby, he thought about what he wanted. There were a few choices in the area. He could go for fast food, which he never ate. Or he could go to one of four pizza shops. Instead, he made his way to The Warehouse to have a nice leisurely lunch. He was even going to read the paper, another thing that he seldom did.

The place was busy when he arrived. The lunchtime crowd was in, and he thought maybe he might not get a table in time. But almost as soon as he started for the door, Thomas, the owner, came to him.

"You're looking very good for a man that nearly died. How are you feeling?" Lucas was being ushered to a table as he answered. "I'm glad to hear that. Cooper and the rest of them, they surely had a hard time of it. You are all very close."

"Yes, we are. We're all we've had for a good many years." Thomas knew what he was and that he was old. "I'm going to start eating. And by that, I mean food that is also good for me. I've been skipping meals in order to work."

"You haven't been in here in some time. And even when you were, you'd be working on that computer that never left your side." Lucas said he wasn't going to worry about things at work when he was away from his desk. "Good for you. My wife, she's got it in her head that I'm going to keel over soon. Got myself on one of them diets that lets you eat all the meat you want. Milly said that I couldn't have bacon at every meal. She's just mean don't you think?"

When he ordered, Lucas looked around while drinking his tea. Thomas had done some upgrades on the place. However, he wasn't going to mention it to Thomas. For all Lucas knew, the upgrades might have been ten or so years ago. He had to think how long it had been since he'd been here and knew that it was at least five years. Christ, he really needed to get out more.

Just as his food was being set before him, he heard a woman shriek. It was a sound that he'd never really heard before but decided that it fit what the sound was. The woman standing there while Thomas talked to her and looked like she could have taken his dragon on and come out a winner.

Watching her carefully, he had the strangest feeling that things were going to go south pretty quickly. There was something...well, unhinged about her. Not crazy, he thought, but she was rabid about something. When her voice rose to a decibel level that he'd never heard before, even his dragon curled away from the sound. Lucas stood up when the woman slapped Thomas.

"Something I can help you with, ma'am?" She turned on him, and Lucas took a step back from her. He was wrong, she was crazy. "Ma'am, there isn't any reason for you to interrupt—"

"Don't you dare call me 'ma'am' again. I'm not old, and I'll never look it either." He didn't have anything to say to that, so he didn't say anything. "I want him to tell me where my sister lives. She's living here, and he claims that he doesn't know her. When I know differently."

"What's her name?" She told him, and it took him a moment to get that straight in his head. "Your sister is Micky Mantle?"

"Our great grandfather loved the football player, or whatever he was, and named her for him. I don't know how Mother and Father allowed that—she's the laughingstock of everyone who meets her. But I want to know where she is." She pulled out a piece of paper and shoved it at his chest. "I've had

23

her investigated. She tells me that she doesn't have any money, and I know better now. She has enough to bail out Bethany. Micky is just being her usual self. A selfish bitch, and I've had enough of it."

"Let me get this straight. You have a sister that is currently in jail, correct? What's your name, by the way?" She told him to pay attention, and then her name. "I am. But you're not making any sense for us to help you with this. You have another sister, one you've had investigated, named Micky. And by the way, Micky Mantle was a baseball player, not football. And on top of all this, you're okay with someone giving you a nickname, but the others around you cannot have the same privilege. That's sort of fucked up, don't you think, Me-Me?"

"I don't give a rat's ass what he was. And I want you to get Micky and bring her to me." Lucas asked her where the elusive Micky lived. "I don't know that. What the fuck do you think I'm trying to figure out? Christ. Were you dropped on your head as an infant? Micky lives around here, but I don't know where. I figured that she'd be waiting tables just to piss me off."

"Why would you care what she does? And why do you make it sound like waiting tables is a sin against you?" She growled, and Lucas laughed again. "You aren't getting anywhere with that attitude. And so you know, I think if she wanted you to find her or whatever, she would have let you know firstly where she lived, and secondly what she did for a living. Why don't you go back to where you came from and leave her and us alone?"

"You'll regret this." He said that he already did, and it was her fault. "My fault? You can't be serious right now. This is all on Micky, and she's going to have to get Bethany out of jail so she can get into the house that her husband owns now and get some items to sell."

"That's called breaking and entering if the house is no longer hers to rule." She growled again. "All right, ma'am, you've worn out your visit, and I suggest you get the rod out of your ass and bend a little."

"So fucking what do I care what the man does for a living? Micky is here, and I want her to come to me this moment. You need to do whatever is necessary to make sure that she pays for this."

Lucas knew that he was going to regret asking the next question, but he had to anyway. "Why is it that you're not paying for it? I mean, Micky doesn't sound like she wants you to find her for the very reason you're needing her found." He looked at her from head to toe and shivered for some reason. "I'd say that you have more than enough funds to pay for Beth to get out of jail."

"Christ. Why do people do that? Her name is Bethany. Micky calls her that too. No matter how many times I tell her not to." Lucas wasn't sure, but he'd bet anything that this Micky called her that on purpose just to piss them off. He was liking this Micky woman more and more. "What are you smiling about? This is serious business here. So, what if her soon to be ex-husband put her there for stupid reasons? And I'm not paying it off, as you so rudely suggested, because I've been put on an allowance for some reason. Not that it's any of your business."

He couldn't help it. Lucas laughed. It felt good too, even at the expense of the woman in front of him getting madder. But when she drew back her hand, to no doubt hit him, Lucas calmly told her that she'd better not.

"I will hurt you if you slap me as you've done to my friend here." Several people around the room snickered. Having enough of this woman, Lucas went to the door and opened it.

Me-Me, whatever that stood for, held her ground and crossed her arms over her chest and began tapping her foot. It was wasted on him, this show of temper. He was a good deal stronger than her, and he had his dragon too. "It's well past time that you moved on. No one would help you now even if you paid them. You're a rude bitch, and I hope to God that you can never find her. Beth and you need to back the fuck off."

When Me-Me went to the door, she turned back and looked at him. Lucas wasn't worried about himself, but he was concerned about what this woman would do to get the information that she wanted. He decided right then to find this Micky person and help her with this mad woman. He reached out to Carson to tell her what he wanted. She, like him, laughed at the whole thing.

All right. I can do this for you, no problem. But I'm also going to check into the others' lives as well. It'll be fun, I think. Lucas told her what he knew for sure. *Well, if she's not waiting tables at Thomas's place, then that's not her occupation. I'll get back to you on this.*

Thanks. I owe you one. And when you find out about this family, I want to know who they're married to as well. I think they should be warned about their plans, don't you? Carson said she did. *Good. I'll be at my office in about an hour. I'm taking an extended lunch, simply because I can.*

She was laughing when he closed the connection with another thanks. There might be something to this, but he had a feeling that it was more than just simple jail time and a sister named Micky. He almost felt sorry for Me-Me when she tangled with Micky. He had a feeling that she could hold her own as much as he could. This was going to be fun.

~*~

Micky dropped all her bills in the mailbox. She was doing good right now. It was the first time in years that she had cash

26

left over from her pay check after paying what she owed, which wasn't all that much. The money that she'd gotten from her grandda when he died was for a rainy day. And there seemed to have not been, thankfully, many of those in a long while.

There was her electric bill, which wasn't much as she was rarely awake when darkness settled in. Her rent was paid up a month in advance. She liked that she'd been able to do that. In case she got behind for some reason, she'd have an extra month to recoup whatever had happened, and for not thinking about the money grandda had given her, Micky was extremely proud of herself.

Walking the rest of the way to work, she thought about her sisters. Beth and Mariam had been so close when they'd been younger. Micky had been left to her own work and play time when they'd go out. Not that they were that much older than her — two and four years respectively. But they, along with their mother, had treated her like she'd been collected from the doorstep and was not really a part of their group. Her mother had told her once that had she known where to have it done, she would have aborted her long before she took her first breath. After that, Micky did whatever she wanted and needed to get out of the house.

At seventeen she left home for good. Micky had been establishing herself some credit long before she should have been allowed to. The local bank manager had let her open a checking account in her name only and gave her a credit card that would be taken out of the account when she used it.

It had taught her a great many things, having a checking account. The most important of them was not to let her newly established credit card out where any of them could see it. It had cost her a great deal of time and money to pay the balance off, and after that, Micky moved again, this time without telling them where she had gone.

Micky clocked in seven minutes before her shift was to begin and pulled her clean smock over her head. It was going to be busy today. The first of the month was always gray day. The elderly would get their checks or whatever money they got, and they'd come in to fill their pantries once again. She loved this part of the month. Micky loved seeing the people coming in.

At lunchtime she went to get some food. It was a splurge, a treat for having money left over this month. Of course, that didn't mean that she'd splurge every day, but she so wanted a Reuben to fill her belly.

Sitting down, Micky told the waitress that she was on her lunch hour, and Sarah said she'd hurry it up for her. Looking around, she decided that Thomas's was a good place to have a treat.

There were tables for the romantic people. Small tables that sat in the back of the restaurant where prying eyes could not see them. There were also tables for the rowdy type. Men and women could come in and sit at the bar while a game was on. And then there was the middle of the place, where she was currently sitting.

Tables for couples or families were spread out so that they weren't too close to each other. When she'd been out once before, at a different place, the man at the table next to hers had knocked her chair every time he moved. Micky loved that it couldn't happen to her here.

Just as her food was set in front of her, a beautiful woman sat down in her booth with her. Micky didn't bother asking her what she wanted, or even why she'd sat down with her when there were plenty of other seats. Instead of that, she ate her sandwich.

"You're very calm, aren't you?" Micky looked at her and

shrugged. "Yes, you're just as I'd been told, beautiful and quiet. You work hard, and you pay your bills on time. Almost the moment you receive them. What some might not know, and I've only just scratched the surface of you, is that you're extremely smart. Like the highest IQ testing that there is."

"Good for you. I mean, you seem to know a great deal about me. For what reason, I don't care. I just want to enjoy my sandwich and go back to work." The woman frowned at her. "This is my seat, miss. And you're —"

"Your sister is looking for you." Micky put her sandwich down, no longer wanting it. "She's figured out that you don't work here, but that you're living in this town. I've had both your sisters investigated — you as well. Also, your mother. How the hell did you survive them when you were a child?"

"I didn't. Once I figured out that I could do better on my own, I took off. I cut them out of my life as best I could." The woman nodded and said that she'd learned that as well. "Why do you care? Not that I really care that you've looked into my life, but why did you do it?"

"My brother-in-law and Thomas, the owner of this place, had a run in with your sister Me-Me the other day. Christ, she's a handful, isn't she?" Pushing her plate away, Micky just wanted to leave. "She had her attorney look for you. Of course, all he could find, and what tripped me up a little, is that you're a female named after someone famous."

"My great grandfather. He named me that when it was undecided by my parents if they were going to keep me. He took me in for the first few years of my life. And when he passed away when I was nineteen, I inherited his estate." The woman nodded. "Who are you? And why do you want information on me?"

"Carson Manning. I'm married to Cooper Manning. Have

29

you heard of them?" Micky told her you'd have to be stupid if you didn't know who the Mannings were. "Yes, we get that a lot. But as I said before, one of my brothers-in-law had a run in with your sister and wanted to know what sort of person they were hunting for. I was asked to find out what I could. Imagine my surprise when I found out that you work at the grocery store. And that you've been there for the last five years. Why are you ringing people out when you could be doing much better using some of your talents as a mathematician?"

"I didn't like that I had to be indoors all the time to work. And even with my education, men treated me like I was an anomaly instead of their equal." Carson told her that she'd had that trouble as well. "I like working for Tim. He's a good man and he runs a nice place."

"He does. But back to Mariam—she's out to find you so that you can pay bail on your other sister, Bethany." Micky told her what she called them. "I love it. If I ever meet up with them, that's just what I'm going to call them."

"I still don't understand why you're here." A plate of food was set in front of Carson and she began eating, telling Micky to finish her lunch between bites of food. Micky picked up her Reuben and bit into it. "I love coming here for this sandwich. I think it's the best treat a woman can have."

"You have the money to do more. I'm wondering why you don't. You have a considerable amount of money in three different banks, a sizeable inheritance from your great grandfather, yet you treat yourself like you don't have anything." Micky told her that it was none of her business. "True. But I was only asking because your sisters, and I would imagine your mother, think that you've not a pot to piss in. Yet here you are, a billionaire several times over. And working a job that you're good at, but it's unnecessary."

"To you it would be. You're sitting here in your four-hundred-dollar dress, shoes that cost enough to feed several people, and a handbag that is worth more than your outfit. I might be someone that works in a grocery store, ringing out people that have considerably less fortune than I do, but they, unlike my family, like me."

Micky stood up and so did the woman. When she spoke, Micky turned her back on her. She didn't need any more shit right now. Her family was going to make things difficult. Not that they hadn't before, but she was just too exhausted to deal with anymore.

"I'm sorry, Micky. I didn't mean to offend you. Not at all." Micky looked at Carson. "I'm truly sorry for hurting your feelings like that."

"In order for you to hurt me, Mrs. Manning, means that I'd have to care. And I don't. Not about you, my family, or anything else. I'm quite capable of taking care of myself. I have been for a great many years."

Micky left the restaurant after paying her bill. As she clocked back in, she decided that she needed to move on. There wasn't a thing holding her here, so she could pack up what little she had in an hour or so and find another place to be. The trouble with that was, she liked it here. It had become a place to call home, something that she'd never had when growing up.

Standing at her station again, she smiled and pretended there wasn't a thing wrong, which she supposed was the biggest lie she'd ever told herself. Nothing was going well. Her family always made sure of that. What she didn't understand was why they did this to her. As far as she could remember, she'd not had a lot of contact with them, and hadn't ever needed anything from them. Yet they treated her as if she was a horrific person, and selfish. Micky didn't understand.

When the man put his things on the line she was in, Micky told herself that she was going to quit at the end of her shift. There wasn't any point in working much longer. And the sooner she got moved, the sooner— She realized that the man was staring at her oddly.

"I'm sorry. Did you say something to me?" He shook his head and she started ringing up his things. A health nut came to mind when she rang up salad makings, coconut milk, and vitamins. When she was finished and told him how much it came to, he stared at her as if he'd never seen a woman before. "Are you all right?"

"I am now. What's your name?" She pointed to her name badge, thinking that he was off his noodle. "My name is Lucas Manning. And you're my mate."

Micky could have gone her entire life without those words. So as soon as he paid for his food, she turned and went to her locker. It was time to go and see another part of the world. Micky would call Tim in the morning. Luckily, she was off for the next two days, and that would give him plenty of time to replace her.

When she came out of the employee break area, the man was standing there waiting. His bags were gone, so she figured that he'd had them taken or he'd simply decided not to bother. Ignoring him, she went out into the blistering heat and started for home.

Chapter 3

Lucas didn't talk to her as he followed her. He knew that she was upset about something, but he was sure that it had nothing to do with him. Or so he hoped. Lucas reached out to Carson, who had been working on things for him for a couple of days and had told him about this woman. Right now, he was drawing a blank on what she'd told him.

You're kidding me? She's your mate? I'm so happy for you both. I think you guys will work well together. By the way, I had lunch with her today. She's sort of touchy about shit, but I liked her. And I respect her as well. Where are you right now? He told her that he didn't know, but he thought they were headed to her house. *I would imagine so. She doesn't live far from work. There is a lot about her that you don't know. Well, that's a given. But her family are some nasty people. She's washed her hands of them, but they don't know how to take no for an answer. They want money. And she has it, too.*

I don't know what I'd do if a mate came to this family who didn't have family problems. Do you suppose the fates are telling us something? About how good we've had it so far? He snorted, and that had Micky looking at him. *She has a fire in her eyes that has my dragon frightened of her just a little. Like he's really glad that she's not a dragon right now so she can't hurt us.*

I'd say that's about right. There are a couple of things that I'm working on for her. Her fiancé died three days before they were to be wed. While it was ruled as suicide, something about it has me looking deeper. Since his death, she's become somewhat of a recluse. Lucas asked her how long it had been. *Seven years. They had filled out all the paperwork for her to receive his insurance before he was killed. Even going so far as to putting in a rider that said that if either of them were to die before they were wed, the insurance pay off would be the same.*

Do you think that her family had anything to do with his death? How did he die? I'm sure you know. She told him that she was looking into it, but the death certificate said hanging. *So, they're thinking that he killed himself, correct? What makes you think otherwise?*

They were in front of a building that had seen better days. However, the yard was cleaned up and had flowers bobbing in the slight breeze. The shutters on the windows had been recently painted, and he could smell that there were herbs around too. He could smell lavender and basil as he walked up the stairs.

"What the hell do you think you're doing?" Lucas wasn't sure how to answer her, so he just told her that he wanted to talk to her. "I'm talked out today. I met your sister-in-law, I'm assuming. She had all kinds of things to tell me too. And other than this mate thing, why is it you think following me is going to get you—?"

The shout in his head from Winnie for them to take cover nearly had him crying out in terror. But grabbing Micky and taking them both to the porch was all he could think about. Then a spray of bullets ran over the wall they'd just been standing in front of, which had him holding Micky closer. Winnie, dragon

34

protector, had just saved Micky's life.

Micky didn't move but held onto his shoulders as he lifted his head from hers. She wasn't injured as far as he could see, but she was far from all right. She was terrified of what had just happened, he was sure. Lucas laid his forehead on hers and tried to calm his pounding heart.

"I'm okay." He told her that he wasn't. "I'm sorry, but you're too heavy. I need to move."

"I'm sorry, but I was shot recently. I just need another moment before I feel like I can sit up." When she nodded, Lucas closed his eyes as he continued. "I have another sister-in-law— her name is Winnie—who is the protector of our kind. She's married to my brother, Hudson. She has the ability to see into the future a little, and that's how I knew to take you down. I'm terribly sorry if I hurt you."

"You're the guy from the bank. The one that was shot in the chest, aren't you?" He said that was him. "I'm assuming that a great deal of you being hurt was for the press. What are you, anyway?"

"Dragon. And yes, a lot of it was for the newspaper and such." Lucas rolled to his back and lay there. When Micky leaned over him he told her that he needed a few more minutes. "I don't know what just happened, but I'm sure that Winnie knows. If you don't mind, I'll speak to her now. All right?"

Micky nodded and asked him if he wanted to come into her apartment. Lucas had no idea why he thought this, but he was sure that she didn't invite people in very often. If ever. When he was seated in the large open area where the kitchen, living room, and dining room all shared the same space, he decided that he liked it. Lucas reached out to Winnie when Micky sat beside him and asked her what she knew.

Her family did this, believe it or not. Why the fuck do people think

35

that the only solution is to kill someone? There is some big fuckery going on, I'm sorry to say. He repeated what Winnie said to him word for word. *Hey Lucas, if she's your mate, tell her to make a connection with me on her end and I can speak to you both. It's a trick I just found out about.*

Lucas told Micky what she needed to do and how to do it and felt her enter the link like she'd been doing it forever. Winnie told Micky what she was, the protector of all dragons, which included her now that she had been found by one of the Mannings.

I'm not sure how I feel about that, but I'd like to know what makes you think that anyone in my family had anything to do with what happened here. Not that I don't think you're right, but what do you know, please? Winnie laughed, and he could feel how much she was liking Micky. *I can see my mother doing this, but as far as I know, no one but a very small group of people knew where I lived.*

It was her and another woman that I can't seem to get a hold on. This other person has too much going on for me to sort out right now. But they're out for your ass too. I'm working on that one. Micky thanked her. *Don't thank me yet, Micky. You've yet to meet me and know what sort of person I am. I might just scare the shit out of you.*

And you don't think being shot at just now was right up there with the freaky shit you might have? Winnie told her that she was sorry. *Don't be. I'm not a fragile cookie like my family thinks I am. Nor am I a pushover. And they're about to find out just how much of a real bitch I can be.*

Both he and Winnie laughed. And when Winnie invited her to dinner, saying that the family was getting together, Micky asked her why she'd need to meet them all. It was scary, really, that she was taking this all so calmly. He reached into her mind and found that it was all an illusion. She was as stressed out about this as he was. When Micky said that she'd come but not to expect too much, Lucas said he'd take her there.

When they closed the connection, Micky got up and started walking around the room. Leaning back on the couch, he was comforted by the fabric and the way the cushions seemed to wrap him up in them. Micky was the best distraction for him. The couch was only making it better.

"I was almost married once. Richard was a good man, but he hung himself right before the wedding. My family said that he did it because he figured out what a loser I was and how he could have done much better. This was just hours after I found his body. Needless to say, I had a time there when I believed them. Then I grew some balls and stiffened up my spine about them." Lucas asked her what she thought of his death. "That it was staged for it to look like he killed himself. Richard would never have done anything like that. He and I were both happy to be getting married, and I had already moved in with him before all that. Plus, there was the note he left behind."

"I'm guessing that you don't believe he wrote it on his own." She said nothing and went to the bookshelf and pulled an old copy of something down. When she handed him a small sheet of paper, he read it twice before he realized what he was reading. "This isn't a suicide note, but more like a grocery list of things that has been written out. They're even numbered."

"Yes, I'm particularly fond of number six, where he tells me that one more of his reasons for killing himself was how I treated my family. And that I should do better helping them out." He read that one and the one after it twice more. "Richard didn't like my sisters. He'd never met my mom, so that was something that was wrong about it as well. Mariam the Second, what I call my eldest sister, said that she'd seen the note in our bedroom before the police arrived. That's how she told me she knew that his dying wish was for us to be a happy family. And for me to share my good fortune with them. She'd been out of the state when he supposedly killed himself, but I could never get her to admit to lying about it."

"I take it that one or both of your sisters wrote the note." Micky said that it was written by Richard, but she thought that someone was making him. "I see. So, this man is set to marry you, and suddenly figures out that you're not right for him and hangs himself. My question would be, why couldn't he have just broken it off or left the area? Any or all of those would have been better than killing himself. Why didn't the police see that?"

"They saw what they wanted to and closed the case. I have thought for a while that Mariam the Second had something to do with that as well. But I can't prove anything." He told her that he'd have Carson or Winnie look into that. "It's doubtful after all this time that there would be anyone that even remembered him. I believe that they all three had something to do with it, and I will until the day I die. This is one of the main reasons that I don't have a thing to do with them."

"There are some things that you must be made aware of. One of them is that since I've touched you when I pulled you to safety, you became an immortal. Just as I am." That had her sitting down hard on the floor. "I'm sorry to have broken it to you this way, but I think it'll help you in the long run in dealing with them."

"Are they as well?" Lucas told her that they would be just as easy to kill as anyone else. "What else do I need to know about you? If we were to come together, that is."

"You'll have magic. I'm not sure what it might be, but you'll take it from me. Also, Cooper, my eldest brother, will share since he's the king of dragons. He'll give you a bit of himself as well. Again, I don't know what that'll entail for you, but you'll have it." She nodded, and he continued. "I'm a very old and extremely wealthy man. Which also, as soon as we touched, became your wealth as well. And on a sour note, I'm sorry, but we can't have children of our own. Not ever. I'm not like other shifters in that they were born a human and can change into their other self. I was born a dragon and have been given the gift of shifting to a man. We, my brothers and I, are the last of our kind."

"You say brothers. How many do you have? So far I'm heard about three of you guys." He told her. "Six dragons, and no one noticed this before?"

"Some know. The townspeople know a little, but they don't say anything. We've provided them with a good life, a safe one too. I guess you could say that we're keeping things on the up and up." Micky asked him if he burned the ones that disagreed with him. "No, I give them two chances, then I crisp them up."

They were both laughing when he heard back from Cooper this time. First, he congratulated him on finding his mate, and then brought him up to date on what he'd done to ensure their safety.

Your house is now fully secure. I took the liberty of doing that when I heard from Winnie. She said that you'd been shot at. Will there be a time when you're not making people want to shoot you on sight? He was joking, and Lucas laughed, but his heart wasn't in it. *I'm sorry. I was just worried about the two of you and her family.*

It's fine, Cooper. You have to know that I was scared to death when I heard the bullets coming at us. I only just got her down under me when they sprayed over the walls. Speaking of which, can you send a crew over here to clean this up? I'll pay for it. Cooper said that he had a crew on their way there now. *Thank you. We're coming to Hudson's for dinner tonight. Winnie said that you all would be there. Have you heard?*

Yes, we're supposed to meet Micky en masse. I hope we don't run her off right away. You know as well as I that we can be quite boisterous when we're all together like this.

Lucas told him that it would be fine. *She's stressed out but hiding it well. I've told her only what she's asked me about. What she would gain from our relationship, and that she's an immortal. Her first question to that was, would her family be as well. When I told her no, Micky relaxed a bit.*

Cooper said that he knew that Winnie and the others were looking into things, and that they'd have more information when he got to the house. Thanking his brother, he told Micky what he'd been told. He explained to her that he couldn't and would never lie to her and wouldn't hold things back from her either.

"I appreciate that. But if I ever ask you if a certain bit of clothing makes my ass look big, you're never to answer that question truthfully." He told her that he thought she had a fine ass anyway. "Flattery will *not* get you laid. Just giving you a heads up on that."

"You can't stay here. I'm sure you know that." She nodded and looked around the small place. "You can stay with Cooper or one of the other married brothers but staying here will get you hurt. And I would very much like to avoid that."

"Why one of your married brothers?" He told her. "Ah, I see. The jealous type, are you? I'm not sure why you'd feel that way about me, but I don't fuck around. Not even with you, even if you are my mate."

"A man can only try, my dear." She smiled at him, and he felt as if the sun was shining only on them. Clearing his throat, he spoke again. "You can pack up some things to take tonight. I'll have someone come in and take care of the rest in the morning. What of this is yours?"

40

"Nothing. It was furnished when I got here. I've liked that, I guess. Every couple of years they upgrade the furniture, and every four change the carpets. It's been a dream living here. Where do you live?" He told her that he'd had a house for a while now and he liked it. "You think that I will if I move in with you?"

"If you don't, then we'll sell it and move to something better. The only request I have is that it's close to my brothers. I need them like I need air. They're all I have besides you." She told him that it wouldn't come to that, she was sure. "All I hope for is for you to be happy. That's my goal in life right now. And keeping you safe."

Nodding, she went to the only other room in the place other than the bathroom. When she came out, she had a suitcase and a duffle. He took them both and asked her what else she needed here.

"Nothing. I mean, there is food in the cabinets. If you could have someone donate it to someplace, that'll be fine. And I'll live with you, but only live there for the time being. I still don't know that this is going to work out for either of us." He told her that he'd work on that. "You don't have to. Just be yourself. I think that's all I want for now."

He decided that he would be himself, and show her the sides of himself that he rarely let anyone else see. Lucas doubted that his brothers saw him as he did himself. No one did. But he'd let Micky see him, and hope that she'd not run in the other direction.

~*~

Me-Me looked at the newspaper, trying hard to find out if the men that she'd hired had indeed killed Micky. Going over it once again, she convinced herself that the paper had come out before they had caught up with her. Micky needed to pay

41

attention to her, or there was going to be trouble. When her name was called to go to see her sister, she stood up and fixed her clothing. It still stung her that the man at the liquor store had asked her if she had a senior discount card.

"I most certainly do not. I'm not nearly old enough for that." And she wasn't. She was just shy of her thirty-fifth birthday. "Where is your manager? I'd like to explain to him how rude you were to me."

When the manager dragged his ass to the cash register, there were several people in line behind her. They were telling her to get over herself, to let it go. But she couldn't. There wasn't any way that she was going to allow anyone to treat her this way.

After telling him that the boy had called her an old woman, the manager just looked at the kid. He told him that he'd only asked her if she had a senior discount card, but he hadn't said a thing about her being old.

"And how is that not calling me old? I just turned twenty-five, you insolent person. You should be nicer and more observant to those around you." Me-Me had been taking ten years from her age since she was actually twenty-five. Someone from the back of the line told her to practice what she preached. Then the manager asked for her driver's license. "I will not allow you to have that. It has my address on it, and anything else that someone like you could use."

"Someone like me? And what, exactly, do you mean by that?" She told him a pervert. "I'm no more a pervert than you are twenty-five. I'm thinking that that boat sailed a long time ago. Now, either show me your license to make this purchase or get out of my store. You're holding up the line and making a nuisance of yourself."

"A nuisance? Me? No, it's you that is causing a ruckus. I demand that you give me a discount on my purchase and have

42

that boy tell me he's sorry." The kid laughed and told her, with a gleam of wickedness in his eyes, that he was sorry that he'd thought she was much older than she looked. "That is not a proper way to say it. I demand that you do this right and tell me that you're genuinely sorry for saying such a thing to me."

In the end she was asked to leave the store. And when she didn't, the police showed up and escorted her, none too gently, out to her car. When she left the lot, she peeled rubber and nearly hit one of the stupid cops with her wheel. Too bad she had missed. It was something she would never forget. She'd just take her business elsewhere from now on.

When her sister was seated across from her, she barely recognized her. Someone had blackened her eye, and her hair looked as if a rat had taken up residence there and was moving in his cousins and all the other rats he knew. They weren't allowed to touch, but she did tell her that she was sorry and asked her if she needed a brush.

"No, I don't need a brush, Me-Me. I need to get out of here. Two of the reprobates cornered me last night and beat the shit out of me for no reason at all. They said that I was making trouble for the rest of them by being rich. Well, that's not what they said, exactly, but you understand what I'm going through. And the guards here are saying that I will have to go before a judge to get my sentencing taken care of. I might have to pay a huge fine for what they consider trespassing." Me-Me told her that she was so sorry, but she'd only just found Micky. "And what did she have to say about helping her sister out? I bet she told you off, didn't she?"

"I'll have you know that she'll never get to do that. But I've not actually spoken to her since the phone call when you were first arrested. And every time I think of that call, I get all the madder at her. Who does she think she is, treating me that way?" Bethany pointed out that she was the one in jail. "Yes, yes, I know that. But I'm the one dealing with her. And she's being as elusive as ever. I swear to you, Bethany, she isn't going to get away with treating the two of us like we're nothing. What does it matter to her if she has to fork over a few hundred dollars? She did get all of Great Grandda's money and stocks. She's probably squandered it all away by now, anyway. Maybe that's why she won't help."

"She has always been tight with her money, Me-Me. I'm sure that you're wrong about that. And she had a way to turn her money into more, while you and I were struggling on budgets as well as alimony checks. Micky has no idea what we go through every day with the restrictions that are put on us. Why, the month before he filed for divorce from me, my credit cards were voided and I couldn't have my jewels unless I asked for them to wear. Who cares if they were his mother's? I love wearing them. And as his wife, he should have wanted me to have them anyway. Who is he going to give them to but me? I know that he'll never marry again."

Me-Me glanced around the area. At least they weren't behind glass walls when they spoke. Most of these criminals should be, just to be sure that they'd not hurt people like her. She looked back at her sister when she said her name.

"David told me if I would promise not to come on the property anymore, and to abide by the rules that are in the divorce decree, that he'd give me ten thousand dollars to set myself up someplace other than here. Did you know that he's selling my house? Like I'm not going to be coming back there." Me-Me asked her if she was going to do it. "No. He has a great deal of money, and ten grand isn't enough for me to live like I should be living. To be honest with you, I thought he was going to give me ten grand a month. But it was just the one time, he told me. I hate being in here when he was making plans to hurt me. I don't deserve this, Me-Me. I was a good wife to him. Not like I was to the other four. I tried hard not to spend so much and not to sleep around. That should give me some goodness from his part, don't you think?"

"I warned you about having men come over to your own house. Didn't I?" Bethany nodded and then smiled at her. "What are you thinking right now? I have a feeling that it's going to be good."

"I was thinking that you should call Mom and have her deal with him. She'll get me more money than ten grand, and perhaps some of the other things from the house that I could sell off. She knows people like that, I know she does." Me-Me asked her if she meant robbery. "Yes, I do. She's done it before. And there are a lot of things in that house that are worth more than your husband is."

She didn't like being reminded that Bethany had married better than she had. But she was still collecting money every month from four of her ex-husbands, and that made her by far better off than her sister. Of course, Me-Me was seeing things that had her thinking that she'd not be married too much longer. It was time for her to be looking for another ex-husband. This one had made her sign a pre-nup before they'd been married, but like a fool she'd thought that she could convince Neil that he didn't need to have it any longer. The man was forever pissing her off.

"I'll call Mom when I leave here. They take your cell phone when you arrive at this dreadful place, did you know that?" She shivered when she thought of the germs and bugs her sister probably had by now. "When you get out of here, Bethany, you're going to have to live in a hotel for a while. You more than likely have all kinds of things crawling all over your person.

Have you seen many little creatures since you've arrived?"

"Yes. Yesterday my food was moving. I swear to you, Me-Me, I'm going to sue this place when they let me go. I hate it here." She asked her if her food was really moving. "No, but I thought it was. It was just settling, they told me. The gravy or whatever it was, it was settling over the biscuit that was under it. And don't get me started on the food here. They're making me eat white bread and drink sugary drinks. They're ruining my figure, I tell you. I'll be a fat slob like the rest of them before I'm set free."

Me-Me put her hand on her own waist line. She was getting heavier as well. No matter how much she exercised or dieted, she could not lose the extra around her waist. When she'd gone to her doctor about getting the fat sucked out of her again, he told her that it was a product of getting older. She would continue to put on weight for her golden years. Me-Me didn't take that any better than the boy asking her if she had a senior discount card.

Leaving the jail, Me-Me knew that as soon as she got home she was going to burn her clothing. It was more than likely filled with all sorts of creatures that she didn't want to think about. Just the thought of them made her skin itch. Going to the parking lot, she saw a large truck go by her and thought that the car on it looked a great deal like hers. And when she got to the space where she was sure that she'd parked her car, she found a note attached to a clipboard on the ground.

Picking it up and reading it, she found that she had been had, and by none other than her own husband. He had taken her car from her, in the form of payment for overspending again. She was going to make him pay for this. Walking to the front gate, she thought of all the things she was going to say to him when she got home. Telling the man at the gate her woes, she was surprised when he asked her if she was Mariam Mantle Patterson.

"Why yes, I am. Why did you want to know?" She was thinking that he'd recognized her from someplace that she'd been. But when he shoved a blue stack of papers at her, she had no choice but to take them. "What is this about? I don't want this."

"You've been served."

Since she had no idea what that meant, she tore open the paperwork that had a seal on it that looked familiar. The man was laughing as he told her that he had recorded that she'd taken the paperwork. But she wasn't listening to him. The fucking bastard of a husband, Neil, had filed for a divorce without asking her about it.

"Oh, I hate men." She stomped her feet, and no one even looked in her direction. That pissed her off more. Someone should wonder why a beautiful woman like her was having such a hard time of it. "How the hell do I get home now?"

That question, along with about a million more, came to her as she stood there. She could call a cab, she supposed, but she didn't have any cash. And her credit cards had been destroyed, right in front of her, by her dear soon-to-be-dead husband. The fucker was going to pay for this.

Chapter 4

Mariam hung up the phone after listening to her daughter go on and on about what had befallen her lately. She didn't care, not really. She had her own set of worries. Mariam was a wanted woman, and it scared her to no end to think that she'd be found. She'd been in on a bank robbery that had gone very wrong.

They had been planning to just go in, fire a few times, then take all the money they could. But one of them shot a woman for staring at him. After that, they all four of them shot anything and everything that moved. It was a fucking mess.

Her daughters—at least Me-Me and Bethany—had been a godsend to her. Whenever she had a spot of trouble, one or both of them would come to her aid. Lately, however, they'd been in trouble too, so the money wasn't there this time. She thought of her youngest, Micky. Why she'd allowed her to be given that horrible name was beyond her.

So, what if the grandda had wanted to name her? For a price he could, she'd told him. Mariam assumed it would be something like his wife's name or a pretty flower—not after the name of a long dead ball player. She hated to be near her when her name was called at something. And of course, the more she was embarrassed by her name, the more pleasure Micky found in using it.

The hotel room she was staying in was a dive, not nearly as nice as she would have liked due to lack of funds. Mariam had never forgiven Peter for not fighting harder when the will was read at his grandfather's funeral. His own father had been killed long before she met him. She wondered if he had been like his own father.

As it was, all they'd received was enough to be able to rent the house they lived in, and that hadn't satisfied her at all. She didn't pay Micky for it, and Micky never said anything about it. She was just as stupid as her father. Mariam had wanted the cash, but Micky got it all. And she'd never shared a single dime of it for all these years.

Moving to the couch that was in the one room place, she wondered how she could get Micky to give her some money. Nothing she'd tried in the past had done the job, nor had she been able to get the amount that had been left to Micky. Their part of the will had been read first, and they were all asked to leave as the lawyer finished up with Micky. And of course, Micky had said nothing as she left the office.

Mariam knew that it was a great deal of money. Micky had also inherited his homes, and stocks in whatever business dealings he'd had. His own grandson, her husband, had been happy with what they'd gotten, even if they had to pay rent to Micky. According to the will, their part anyway, they'd *borrowed* enough from the old man to make up for any kind of cash payout to them. They'd never paid him back when they needed cash. And why should they? He was rich, so in turn, she figured they were as well.

"What to do, what to do?"

As predicted by Cain Mantle, the fucking bastard, the marriage hadn't lasted. When the money dried up, she started looking for ways to supplement her lack of cash. Peter hadn't realized that she was doing anything—that was, until the police had come for her. Her sentence for stealing cars, as well as dealing in drugs, had gotten her ten years in jail and a bracelet on her ankle so that she couldn't leave home when she was released. That shit had caused her to miss a lot of parties.

That was the day she'd found out that her husband was having an affair, and that he'd been seeing the woman long before Mariam's arrest. As soon as she was jailed, Peter had finally grown a set of balls and filed for divorce. She got that paperwork while she was sitting in a jail cell. By the time she got out, he'd not only moved out of their rental, but he'd made sure that Mariam didn't know where he'd gone when he left town.

The knock at the door startled her. No one knew where she was except her favorite daughters, and they'd not just show up without telling her they were coming. Sitting as still as she could, she waited for the second, then third knock before moving to the door.

"I know that you're in there, Ms. Mantle. I can smell you." She wanted to tear open the door and slug the man on the other side. But she was afraid of what he might do if she were to come out of her safe haven. "I've been sent here to tell you a few things. And if you're smart, which is doubtful, you'll heed what I tell you. Stay away from Micky. Don't call her, don't talk to her, nor are you to try and harm her. She is with a powerful family now, and you'd do well to leave town before they come for you."

"What kind of person tells me that I cannot see my own

flesh and blood? She's my daughter, and I'll do as I damn well please concerning her." She opened the door then and looked at the man before her. While she didn't know him, she thought that he was quite powerful himself. "You tell my daughter that she needs to come and talk to me. We have a few things to talk about. One of them is giving me a part of what she inherited from that old shit."

"I will relay the message, but I'd not hold my breath on her coming to you. As I said, she is with a powerful family now, and they protect their mates." He smiled at her, and she saw an animal run over his skin. "I'm a wolf. Pack leader to hundreds. If you come onto their land, be assured that my men will tear you into bite sized pieces that will never be found."

"Are you threatening me?" He shook his head and smiled wider; she could see his canines clearly now. "I should hope not. I'm a person that you don't want to fuck—"

"I wasn't threatening you, Ms. Mantle, but telling you the truth. I will sic my pack on you if you so much as touch Micky." He turned then and made his way to the elevator. "I've called the police. There is a fat reward for someone turning you in."

She heard the sirens then. Rushing into the room, she grabbed up her bag that hadn't been unpacked and darted out the door. The single elevator was in use, so she took the stairs. As soon as she opened the door, the sounds in the deep area of the steps sounded and vibrated along the walls and her head. She had just set off the fire alarm. Running faster now, more people joined her on the stairs.

All she could think about was that she could blend in with them. And if she was right, the wolf on the elevator would be stuck there and unable to get out. She knew for a fact that elevators were turned off in the event of a fire, so that no one would try and use them.

As soon as the sun touched her face, she was escorted to the area where all the other people were waiting. The building was being checked, they were told, and as soon as they were assured that nothing was wrong, they'd allow them back in. Mariam decided this was the best time for her to move on, to find a place to regroup and find her daughter, Micky.

There wasn't any money for a good hotel. The one that she finally found only charged her for the one night, and she'd have to pay up when she left the place. She was given a room at the front of the place, on the uppermost level and close to a pop machine and the ice maker. Going into the room, Mariam was immediately engulfed in the charm and luxury of the place. Small towns—you had to love them when they were the only deal in town.

The queen-sized bed in the center of the room was as soft as butter, and there was plenty of space between it and the wall, the room was so big. There was a television on the dresser, with a screen as wide as the bureau, which was saying a lot since it was a large dresser. There were hooks on the wall over the sink that held hand embroidered finger towels that she was going to take with her when she left.

The bathroom too was spacious. The tub and a shower shared the same area, away from the toilet and sink. The commode was one of the larger ones, the kind that were no longer being put into homes, and she was happy to see that it was clean.

While she was sitting there contemplating whether or not she had gotten the wrong room, a godawful noise had her jumping up and plastering herself to the wall. It was the ice machine that someone was using, she figured out later when it sounded again. And the pop machine made a noise like someone was tumbling a large stone down an equally stone mountain. As she was sitting on the bed, three more people got some ice, and two got a drink from the noisy machine. It was, as far as she was concerned, the only drawback to the room.

"Why me?" She knew why bad things happened to her. She wasn't a nice person. And Mariam also knew that she had been that way her entire life. So why change now? "Micky needs to help me. If for no other reason than I'm her mother."

Mariam thought of what the wolf had said to her. Maybe he was telling the truth, or maybe not. Micky could have hired him to act all bad assed and to scare her off. Well, it wasn't going to work. Micky had it all, and she wanted a portion of it. A large portion.

At midnight the music started. She had no idea what type of music it was because the bass was so loud that it vibrated her out of the bed. Sitting on the floor, she wondered when it would stop; or should she just go over there and make them stop? Deciding on the latter of the two choices, she dressed in a pair of lounge pants and a white T-shirt. Mariam was very happy with her outfit. She just loved to show off what she had.

Pounding on the door several times, she finally heard the music being turned down to a more manageable level. Mariam stood there waiting for someone to come to the door when the music was turned up louder than it had been before. Christ, would this ever end?

Pounding again on the flimsy door, she thought about kicking it open. But she didn't know what the people on the other side had as weapons. When it finally opened up, she could only stare at what was going on in the room. Then she noticed the gun pointed right at her.

"I wanted to ask you to turn the music down. I'm trying to sleep." He just laughed, the gun in his hand never wavering. "How long have you been making meth here?"

"Ain't none of your business, I'm thinking. But if the cops so much as do a drive by, you're dead." The second time in two days she'd been threatened with death. "Now normally, I'm not the type of person that would let you live. But I'm feeling pretty good about this project I'm on, so you go on back to your room and forget what you saw."

"What if I were to help you?" He cocked an impressive brow at her, a feat that she'd never been able to master. "I've done this before. I never got caught, but I had to move on when the building I was using burned to the ground."

"You made meth?" She nodded and told him how she had done it, even giving him the names of several brokers, as she called them, that could verify her story. "You hang on a minute. I know one of them guys. Don't fucking move, do you hear me?"

"Yes, I'm sure that the entire hotel heard you." Mariam looked around and saw that other than the men, she was the only one in the place. Not able to see upstairs from her position on the ground, she thought perhaps the men had made that happen.

When he came back, he motioned for her to enter, and the smell in the tight place made her slightly dizzy. Christ, they were making some good shit in here. Looking around at their set up, she noticed that there wasn't a bed in the room, nor any furniture other than what they were using. There was a second door in the room that opened up into the room next to the one they were in. In there she could see more workers and had to hand it to this guy—he had it going on.

They talked about terms, how much she'd get for some work. It wasn't a great deal, but she had to prove herself to him. She was giddy with the idea that she was making a comeback in the world of dope. Mariam gladly donned the clothing that was handed to her so that she wouldn't have her clothing smelling like drugs.

By the time the sun was coming up and glaring into the room through the open curtain, she figured that she'd done a good job for the man. There were no names given, so she kept her own to herself. Standing up, stretching her back and arms, she saw the man looking at her.

"You like what you see?" He shook his head. "Well, that's rude. I wasn't offering it to you anyway. Just asking you."

"Nah, you were hoping for a quick fuck to get you through the day. Sorry, but you're the wrong sex for that to be happening." She stared at him, sure that her mouth was hanging open. "Not all gays wear flamboyant clothing and talk with a lisp. You keep your mouth shut and go back to your place and rest up. We have a large order going out tomorrow, and we're shorthanded."

Returning to her little room, Mariam was too tired to even undress. Taking off her shoes and falling into the bed, she touched her fingers over the cash she'd been given. Five hundred bucks would certainly go a long way to helping her get ahead in the world. Hopefully the little shits next door wouldn't get caught any time soon, and she'd be rolling in the dough. Closing her eyes, Mariam thought about her daughter Micky again.

She was going to pay for this humiliation. As surely as she was lying here, Micky was going to pay her, or she'd rain down a hurt on her so badly that she'd be begging for her to stop.

"Not until I get what I want. She'll have to suffer as I have done. I gave birth to her—the least she could do for that inconvenience is to pay me."

She'd started to fall asleep when the music was turned on again. Instead of letting it bother her, she let it go by putting a pillow over her head. She wasn't going to piss off the man with the money, not now at least.

~*~

Lucas was having a hard time focusing on anything. Not just his work, but even when he was getting dressed this morning, he'd literally forgotten how to tie his shoes. Stretching again, trying to work on the kinks in his body, he looked up when Alan came in the room.

"You didn't tell me that you had such a pretty mate." He said that he thought her to be gorgeous. "She is. And she's here."

He looked at the doorway and then back to Alan. Why was she not in here where he wanted her to be? Lucas asked him what she wanted.

"To have a conversation with you. But she wouldn't just barge in, even though I told her that you were getting no work done anyway. Have you read over the proposals that I sent you?"

Guiltily, he told Alan that he'd been distracted. The man laughed and stood up. As he was making his way to the door, Lucas asked him why she'd not wanted to come in.

"She didn't want to disturb your work, nor did she feel comfortable enough to just come in and talk to you. She's afraid that you're a busy man." He told Alan he was. "Not so far as I can see, you're not. By the way, you will have to go to the bank in the morning. There are some papers you have to sign concerning Micky."

When Micky joined him, he noticed that Alan had shut the door behind her. Lucas rarely shut his door unless he was talking to an employee or to a person that needed his help. When she stood in the area halfway between the door and his desk, Lucas stayed where he was. He didn't want to rush her about anything.

"A man by the name of Hank Kent came to see me today. He told me that he had pack on the grounds and that he'd spoken to my mother. Did you send him there?" Lucas told her he hadn't, but he thought that it might have been Carson or Winnie. "I see. Don't you have any say on what goes on around your home?"

"Yes. As do you. But with your mother out there, we're all taking extra precautions. I want you safe." She nodded but didn't move. "Are you planning to leave? If not, I'd like for you to have a seat."

"You want me." There was no point in denying it—he told her that he did want her. "I don't know what to do about that. I'm not even sure that I care for you all that much. I mean, you're a very nice man—well-built and handsome—but I'm...I guess you could say that I'm slightly overwhelmed by you."

"Is it because of what I am or something else?" She said that was part of it; the rest, she told him, was what he wanted with her. "I want nothing that you're not willing to give me, Micky. I do want you, with every fiber of my being. My dragon does as well. But we won't take what is not freely given. Ever."

"I believe you. But I'm still having some trouble figuring out how I'm supposed to fit into your life." Lucas asked her what she meant. "You're wealthy. I've been talking to Carson, and she said that you're all worth billions, as in plural. I have money too—a lot. But I had to ask her if she meant millions, and she assured me that she meant billions. She told me that there was no way to equate how much you had stashed away and in property. But she did tell me that you have more than the rest, simply because you've learned how to invest wisely and didn't mind taking a chance."

"I've done very well for myself. But even if I hadn't, I

58

still have a great deal of money. Money that I've shared with you." She nodded and took two steps in his direction. It was hard for him to be patient — he wanted to hold her that badly. "As a dragon, we can make money from our tears. The story behind that is partially true. Our tears depend on what we are shedding them for. Love, hate, anger, they all have a different hue to them because of it."

"I was going to ask you about that, but I was embarrassed and afraid that you'd be angry with me." He said that he'd never be angry with her, she was his life. "That's the part that overwhelms me. Did you know that the bank called the house? I needed to go there and sign some paperwork. I had no idea that you'd put me on your accounts. Why would you do something like that when you've only just met me?"

"In my heart, you have always been there for me." He moved to the front of his desk, sitting on it while playing with a pen. It was that or he was going to charge at her and take what he needed. "We only get one chance at happiness. And you are mine. When my parents were alive, both of them beautiful strong dragons, we, as their children, could see what they meant to each other. And when my mother was killed, Dad would have joined her that moment, but he had to keep us safe too. That was why he did what he did."

"He changed you." Lucas nodded, but told her that it was more than that. "Can you tell me? I mean, tell me what happened to make you guys so special. Maybe it'll help my stress level right now."

"All right. But come and have a seat, please. It'll be much easier to tell you if I don't think you're making a plan for a quick getaway." She moved across the floor slowly, and Lucas wondered if she knew just how sexy he found that simple movement. When she was seated, he stayed where he was.

They were making progress, and he wasn't messing that up. "Our dad went to see a witch long before the night that he changed us. For a month he practiced and practiced the words that would change us, we were told. My dad was a powerful being — the king of all dragons — so his magic was considerable. But it wouldn't be enough to change all of us at once. The witch, she even lent her magic to him, and still it wasn't enough."

"But they found it elsewhere, I'm assuming. Otherwise you'd not be here today." He told her that was right. "I'm sorry for interrupting you, but I like to ask questions."

"And you should. This is very different than anything that has happened to you before. Taking it in small doses is much easier for me too when I have a difficult task before me." She nodded and told him she was ready for more. "There had been a meeting that night. All the dragons — there were considerably less than there had been the year before — had gathered in the cave. The searcher of our kind, forever trying to find a way for us to fit in with the humans, told us that all dragons were doomed. It was true, his words and my dad's — he knew that he was doomed as well."

"Your mother, what happened to her?" He cleared his throat before answering her. His emotions were so high right then that he could have easily cried on her shoulder. "I'm sorry again."

"Don't be. Please? It's just that I've not thought of this for a long time. But about my mom. I didn't know her as well as the others. Tristan and Xavier even less than that. She was murdered by the humans in the town because they could. She died trying to protect us, by luring away the men that were there to kill us all. And for her sacrifice, we were safer for a little while." He thought of the story that had been told to him numerous times. "The meeting was just about to finish up when our dad came

60

to tell us of our fate. As you can well imagine, we were terrified at what Dad brought back to us in details. He too believed that we were all to die, so he told us what he was going to do and that it would drain him and those still in the caves. They were the extra magic that made it possible for us to walk among the humans and be safe."

"Oh, how lovely. I think your parents should be honored for what they did. They literally gave up their lives for their children. No one does that anymore." He moved to her and wiped at the tears on her cheeks. She looked up at him, and he could see how much his story had moved her. "Tell me the rest, please? I want to know what happened to your dad."

"In giving us all that he had, as I said, it drained him. And as he lay there dying, his heart getting weaker and weaker, we stood around him as our dragons. We thought that it hadn't worked, that we were surely going to be killed like our mother." He stretched out his legs and picked Micky up and sat her on his lap, and when she didn't seem to care, he continued. "Cooper, who is the eldest of us all, he stayed by Dad's side for the entire time, until he took his last breath and his heart beat no more. The faeries knew that a great dragon had died — for his children no less. That was when Rose came to be with Cooper. She was his faerie. But the others, millions of them, picked up our dad and took him to a faerie garden just for him. They laid what they could in the same garden of my mom. I go there sometimes when I want to talk to them."

"Of course, you would. They were very special." She put her arm around his neck and started playing with the hair on the back of his neck. Lucas tried to think what they'd been talking about when Micky spoke again. "How long did it take you to change? I think that's what it's called, isn't it?"

"Yes, that's right." He laughed, remembering the day they'd

left the cave. "We were told that the humans were coming, that we needed to take cover. Running as best we could through the cave, we stumbled out into the sunshine just as it was cresting the mountain that we lived in all those years. Cooper changed first, I think, I don't remember that part now. But we all changed into humans. It took us years to figure out the humans of this world. How to walk like them. Talk as they did. We have, over the years, had to reinvent ourselves. Also, learn things that the rest of the world of people took for granted. Things like eating food, drinking from a glass, things that even any child would be aware of."

"I'm so sorry." He kissed her palm when she touched his cheek with it. Lucas asked her what she was sorry for. "You've had a difficult life. Most people would have crumbled under the pressure that you guys were under. I can't even imagine the things that you went through to be the man that you are. I'm sure that your father and mother are so very proud of what you've all become."

Pulling her closer to him, Lucas kissed her. He wanted it to be gentle, thanking her for her heartfelt words that touched his heart. But the moment that his mouth took hers, he knew that if he didn't stop now, he'd never be able to. Pulling away from her, Lucas looked at her, the dazed look in her eyes—the sadness was there also.

"Lucas, I've fallen in love with you." He told her that he loved her as well. "Will you take me home and make love to me? I want you very badly."

"I want you too. So how about if we start here and then end up at home?" When she asked him how that feat was going to take place, he lifted her up enough for her to turn on his lap. Now her legs were on either side of his, and he could smell her heat. Smell just how much she wanted him. As much as he did her.

Chapter 5

Micky was overwhelmed by the way that she felt for this man. He could easily trample all over her heart and she'd beg him for more. Kissing him while he touched every part of her, Micky cried out when he took her breast into his mouth and suckled hard.

"I need more." She nodded, unsure at this point that she could take any more from him, Lucas stood her up in front of him and ripped her clothing off her. "Yes, this is what I need. To see you."

"I feel so exposed like this. What if someone comes in?" He winked at her and stood up too. Kissing her again, more like devouring her, she didn't care then if the entire room was filled with people watching them. He was making her crazy with need. "Take me, Lucas. I need for you to take me."

"I will, my love. In due time."

He dropped to his knees in front of her, his fingers dancing along her belly just below her belly button. And when he stuck his tongue inside of the small indentation, she cried out with a quick and devastating climax. "I'm going to have you for my meal."

He didn't waste any time on his eating her. Lucas's tongue touched her everywhere. Her naval, her hips—even the backs of her legs were tasted. It was all she could do to stand upright. And when he pulled her nether lips apart and stared at her, Micky felt her body warm, and cream ran down her legs. Then he licked her.

She did more than scream when she came that time. It was as if she blacked out for a moment or two, only to wake to Lucas consuming her over and over. Even as he nibbled at her clit, held her ass firmly in his hands, she came so many times that she was weak with it. Her knees were trembling.

"I have to sit down. Lie down. I don't care, but I can't stand up any more." She felt herself moving, and the couch that she'd sat on a few times was beneath her back. He didn't waste any time in positioning her—he simply stood above her and his clothing disappeared. She'd have to ask him about that later, but now she could only think of one thing as he stood over her. She needed to taste him too.

His cock was thick and long. Every part of his cock was hard as stone. Touching her fingers to the tip, circling the crown as she watched him, she could have come easily again when he moaned for her to take him into her mouth.

Lucas didn't rush her, he didn't take over when she took him into her mouth for a moment. He was a tight fit, and she wondered how he was going to be able to fit within her. But his cock was leaking again, the tip of it flowing with his own cream as she licked him clean. Nothing had ever tasted so good.

"That's it, honey. Taste me. I want to come all over you. Will you let me?" She nodded as she bobbed onto his cock. "Christ, I'm coming."

He pulled from her mouth just as his hot spray of cum

touched her. It was all over her face and breasts. Opening her mouth to catch as much as she could, Micky slid her fingers into her pussy to give herself some relief for what he was doing to her.

Micky found herself on her feet then, her back to him as he told her in a rough voice to bend over. As soon as she was bent at the waist, Lucas didn't just fill her, but he became a part of her. Nothing could have prepared her for the way she felt when he started fucking her from behind. Begging him for more, telling him that she needed him to come, he slid his fingers into her pussy and pinched her clit with his thumb and finger. Micky screamed once again, and then everything just blinked out.

When she woke, she was laying on the couch with him spooned in behind her. Lucas was humming—she thought it was a tune that her great grandfather had listened to. Micky turned in his arms and Lucas kissed her, deeply and full of passion.

"You passed out on me." She smiled at him, not the least bit sorry that she had. "I thought about taking you home, but neither of us were up to getting off the couch, much less me driving a car right now."

"That was epic." He thanked her. "I'm not kidding. I have never come so hard and so many times in all my life. Please tell me that it's not going to be like this every night. If so, then I might just test out my immortality and die a happy woman."

"No, it won't be like this every night." She was both relieved and disappointed. "We'll also be like this during the morning hours, as well as lunch. And if I can work it in, any other time of the day too."

She laughed with him, not sure if he was kidding or not. When she rolled back on her side, his arm wrapped around her, she lay there thinking of all the things that had come to her when she'd met a dragon.

"Your boss called while you were resting. He wanted to know if you were feeling good enough to come back to work. He had some hours to fill if you wanted them." Micky turned again, looking up at his face as he relayed the message. "I've had Carson go there, to check him out and see if he really needed you, and he does. I don't mind that you work—it's your business to do whatever you wish. But I'd ask that you keep an eye out for your family. You do know that they're both in town now. With your sister in jail for trespassing, I'm not sure how they'll react if they see you out in public."

"I'm going to have to talk to them, aren't I?" Lucas told her that it was entirely up to her what she did with them. "What happens if they hurt me, Lucas? How will you take that? Because I'm sure that they mean me harm."

He kissed her on the forehead and told her that he loved her before answering her. "There will never be a hole that they can crawl in, a place locked up where they'll be safe. I will find them and kill them."

Lucas kissed her again, then moved over her to stand up. After helping her stand, she looked at her clothing that laid in tatters on the floor. Looking up at him, she wondered how she was going to leave here when it was time. Micky asked him if he had a shirt she could pull on.

"As far as I'm concerned you could be naked all the time. I'd very much enjoy that." She smacked him on the bare chest, then ran her fingers through that soft fur that he had there. "Your magic will help you with that. Just think of something that you'd like to wear. Even shoes and socks. Anything that you can think of to wear, you can have it on you."

"And since I noticed that you were naked very quickly, I'm assuming that I can undress in the same manner. Would I be able to leave on some of my clothing and remove the rest?" He asked her what she meant. "You know, keeping my dress on but my panties are gone."

He growled at her and Micky felt it over her entire body, like she'd stuck her finger in a live socket and felt the electricity race over her. When she thought of things to wear out of here and to home, Micky was shocked. Even though he'd told her it would happen, she still couldn't believe it.

"We have some things to do today, if you're up to it." She asked him what sort of things. "For one, you have to go to the bank and sign some paperwork. The house and all the other properties that we own will now be in your name."

"No, you can't do that. What if...? I don't know. What if I get some kind of disease and you have to put me down? I'm not saying that right, but I think you understand what I mean." He told her he did, and he laughed. "Hey buddy, I'm as new to this as it was for you and your brothers being human."

"I am profoundly sorry then." Lucas laughed with her. "The reason that we put it in our spouse's name is because we've been around for a very long time. And sometimes we have to reinvent ourselves so that no one notices. The townspeople here, they know what we are, but there are others out there that will hunt us down and try to kill us for being immortal. We are, first and foremost, dragons that could bring them riches beyond what they could dream up. Understand now?" Micky said that she did.

After another kiss on her mouth, Lucas backed away. It was then that she heard the phone chirping. And it really did sound like a bird. When he answered the phone with just his last name, Micky sat down. She supposed she should leave him to his call, but she wanted to be with him as much as she could.

When the call ended, she could tell that something had

happened. Micky didn't know Lucas well enough to gauge his moods, but she was pretty sure that he was upset about something. And for whatever reason, she thought it was her family.

"Can I help you with whatever is going on?" He nodded, but then shook his head. "Lucas, I told you that I loved you, but if you don't allow me to help or to know what you're thinking, I might bash you over the head."

"You're a violent little thing, aren't you? It's your sister, Me-Me. What the hell kind of name is Me-Me anyway?" They chuckled. "She's been served her divorce papers. The paperwork was filed earlier this morning. And Neil, because of his connections, was able to get it taken care of quickly. She is none too happy about any of this. Apparently, he's taken her credit cards, as well as her mode of transportation."

"Do you know where she is? Not that I'm going to help her out of this. If anyone deserved to be left in the cold, it's my sisters. Mother too, but she's a fish of a different color. Meaner and sneakier than both sisters put together." He said that he was beginning to see that. "Where is Me-Me? Do you know? And Me-Me is a nickname that she made up for herself. She claimed, to anyone that would ask, that she did it to make it so that people knew she was the younger of the two of them. They both, Mother and Mariam the Second, dress like they're still in high school. They also believe that they have the bodies to go along with it. Neither of them have taken a good look in the mirror for a long time, I'm thinking."

"She's currently trying to find someone that will lend her a car. And while she's at it, she's asking anyone that crosses her path if they know where you are. She was hanging out at the library but made a nuisance of herself when she kept throwing books to the floor when they weren't what she wanted to read.

As you can well imagine, she didn't like being escorted from there any more than she did being barred from the local car dealership. He said that she'd tried to have sex with him in exchange for a car." Micky told him that it had gotten her what she wanted for a long time when they were younger. "Christ, how can you possibly be from the same family as them?"

"Just unlucky, I guess." Going to the window, she stared out at the scene below them. The place that was right behind this building was beautiful. It was a park she'd bet anything that Lucas had put in so that he'd have something better to look at than falling down buildings. Kids and older people were there to feed the pigeons and relax. She could see the workmen in one part of the park putting in a space for walkers and jogging. "I talked to Carson this morning after you left to come here. She asked me all kinds of questions about Richard. And about my great grandda. She said that she was digging as deeply as she could. And she was enjoying it."

"That sounds like her. Carson loves a challenge. I'm sure that Winnie is working with her as well. Grace will be cheering them on as they think up and discard many plans. I don't ask. They're scary by themselves, but together they're terrifying."

"Would you put me in that group too?" She didn't look at him, fearful of what she might see there. When he didn't answer her, she glanced at him and asked again.

"I think you're much stronger than you think you are. Or have even give yourself credit for. You have enough sense to save and to invest for yourself. And to stay away from your family." She told him that she wasn't all that strong. "Oh, but you are. And you're getting stronger every day. Standing up for yourself, as well as not taking any shit from anyone. I heard that you got on Cooper's ass this morning too."

"He was driving me nuts with all his vague answers and

71

complicated questions. Just fucking say what you mean. Don't go about the story so that it has so many twists and turns that you completely lose focus on what it is he was talking about in the first place." Lucas said that was him in a nutshell. "And he showed me his daughter. Wow, she's going to be a heartbreaker when she gets older. She's beautiful."

"She is. And there isn't one of us that wouldn't do anything in the world for her." She moved to sit on his lap again. Micky had never been one to snuggle and hug someone, but she wanted that from Lucas. When he wrapped his arms around her and held her tightly, she thought about all the shit that had been going on in the last few years.

"My mother has been arrested before. That was when she was divorced from my father. He died a few years later, a happy man I think. He remarried almost right away, but he'd been so unhappy that I couldn't help but be happy for him when he left." Lucas asked her what her mother had been arrested for. "She was dealing drugs. Making them too, I found out. The only reason that she got out early was that she gave up the crew of men that worked with her and for her. There was quite a long list of unsolved deaths that she was able to help them with too. That sounded like something she'd do—rat out people and make sure her hands were never dirty."

"She sounds like a great role model for kids." Micky laid her head on his chest—hearing his heart beating made her sleepy. "What about your great grandda? I think his name was Cain?"

"Yes it was. I didn't really have enough time with him. He was a large part of my childhood in that I'd hear so many stories about him, and I lived with him for a time. He was the one that named me. And I'm so happy that he did." Lucas asked her how old she was when he passed away. "Nineteen. I had come home from classes and he wasn't up yet. In my head I knew what had happened, but it took my father to get me to listen to what he had to say to me. He said that Grandda had died in his sleep with a smile on his face. And one of my drawings in his hand."

She thought of that when she was thinking of her great grandda. He had told her every day that he loved her with all his heart. That the only part of him that she didn't own was the part that he had for his dearly departed wife. Micky had been so proud to be thought of so highly, and she felt that she was in good company sharing his heart with Great Grandma.

~*~

Me-Me was pissed off. She'd been treated so horribly that she wasn't sure who to blame it on at the moment. People were just plain mean to her, and she didn't understand what she'd done to make them treat her like she was a second-rate citizen. Maybe even lower than that.

Like the library. What was the man's beef about her tossing books off the table where she'd been sitting? It wasn't like it wasn't his job to clean up after people. What the hell would you need him around for if not to do just that? And besides, she thought that she should be applauded for helping the community by keeping people busy.

Her husband had filed for divorce, and she'd not even had time to try and convince him otherwise. It was a done deal. Calling him had done her no good either. He had changed the number already, and she couldn't get the operator to tell her what his new number was. Even under threat of messing her up, she firmly told Me-Me that he had made his number private for a reason. Perhaps, but she wasn't the reason, surely.

On top of all this, Micky was still alive. She was like a fucking cat, having more lives than anyone she'd ever heard of. But she wasn't giving up on things. Me-Me had figured out when she'd been tossed from the library that when Micky was dead, the money that she had would come to her and her sister. Mom too, but since she was in deep shit, she'd not need any of it while in prison.

She'd been wondering about other things too. She used to be so good at thinking outside the box, but she'd almost forgotten that she could do this. There was plenty of time for her to do it. Thinking on her feet and planning for herself was what had gotten her where she was today.

"Well, not today, but in the past." Dialing the last phone number that she'd had on her husband before Neil, she met with a dead end there as well. He too had changed his number, and set it to private. "How the hell did they turn against me all at once?"

Me-Me needed her mom. She would have something stashed away for a rainy day. And even if she wouldn't share, she'd have a place for Me-Me to rest up and get a shower. Not having a bath in three days made her sick of her own odor. And she was itching all the time too.

Positive that she'd gotten some kind of bug when she'd been visiting Bethany, Me-Me decided that she wasn't going to go and visit her any more. Helping her was still on her list, but she'd have to do it from afar. Maybe if she could get enough money together, she'd have someone go there only to slip her a cell phone. That way they could talk without her actually being next to her and her nasty creepy things.

Of course, she'd need a phone of her own too. Hers had been shut off a few hours ago. It had taken her most of the rest of the day to find out that it wasn't broken, but that the service had been turned off. Her husband again. Christ, he was a pain in the ass.

"I didn't want to be married to him any longer anyway."

She kept telling herself that over and over until she believed it. All the perks that she'd had going for her were gone. He'd taken her livelihood and extras, all in one fell swoop. "And I didn't even get to have anything from the place that I could sell off either. Damn that man. I'm betting that he and Bethany's husband got together to ruin our plans."

If she was honest with herself, which she rarely was, she'd forgotten how smart Neil was. When she met him, he'd been at a party with a date. Not that another woman would bother her overly much. She'd been wrecking homes long before there was a name for it. And she loved it.

But Neil had made her sign the pre-nup. He'd also given her an allowance that she was to abide by or funding would be cut off. The first month of their marriage she'd gone over her limit by quite a bit, and for the next three months Neil had taken half her allowance to pay it back. After that, Me-Me was very careful not to go over. That lesson had hurt her badly with her friends.

"Like any of them are true friends." Me-Me had called several of the women that she'd always had lunch with, ones that were just as snotty as she was. But they turned their back on her, one of them even going so far as to tell her that she wasn't to call her ever again. That hurting Neil was just wrong on so many levels.

Walking everywhere was hurting her feet. And it was so fucking hot out that she was sure that she was going to be sunburned if she didn't get a car soon.

Just as she was going to sit down on one of the many park benches on the main street, she saw Micky. It took her several moments to realize who she was, but anyone would have had a time of that. Micky looked different. She actually thought that she was glowing. And the man with her, tall and well built, was holding her hand and talking to her closely.

"Micky has a boyfriend." Saying it out loud didn't make it any less real for her. If this was going to lead to a wedding, then she and Bethany would be fucked over when Me-Me killed her sister. The money would assuredly go to him and not them. "What the hell could he see in her? I mean, just look at her."

Me-Me did and wasn't pleased with what she was seeing. Micky's clothing was beautiful. Her hair was done up in a single braid that hung down her back, with streaks of added color in it—a wide stripe of blue, no less. Even from where she was sitting, she could see that Micky had grown up to be very pretty. Not as pretty as her, but she could pass muster if she were pressed to be with her.

The man with her kissed Micky, a long drawn out one that she found herself envious of. Micky and this man, they were in love. When he moved on down the street, Micky entered the grocery store. When she didn't come out right away, Me-Me moved to get a better look inside.

And there she was, running the cash register, and having a good time at it as well, laughing with the low-lifes that came in. It would be just like her to cozy up to one of them and have them give her whatever she wanted. Not that they'd have anything from the looks of them, but it wouldn't bother her sister. She had always liked being with people that were so much beneath them that Me-Me wanted to hit her.

She thought about going inside and confronting her sister. Me-Me figured that if she had a job then she'd have cash. But she did worry about her having a job and the meaning behind it. Me-Me knew as surely as she was sitting there that Micky had done just what she'd predicted. The money was gone.

Standing up, gathering a little more courage, she went into the store. Micky looked at her, right in the face, but turned to talk to the woman in line. That infuriated Me-Me to no end, to be ignored by someone less than her.

"You have any money on you, Micky? If so, I want you to give it to me. I need some, and I, as your sister, think you should just fork it over. I don't have time for your shenanigans today either. I'm hot and tired, and my husband left me stranded." Micky shook her head and said no. Just like that, *no*. "Micky, I'm not kidding you. I need some money. I have no idea why Neil divorced me, and now I'm not even able to stay in my home."

"I'm busy here. Why don't you go get it off of Mother, or even Beth? Oh, I remember, one is in jail and the other one isn't that far behind. What about you? You ready to go to the big house?" It infuriated Me-Me that Micky would bring that up in front of someone else, much less a crowd of people that were less than nothing to her. "Go away, Mariam, before I call the police. I don't have time to mess around with you. And even if I did, you'd not be any better off in getting money from me. Never again."

The line of people had never stopped moving, Micky continued to do her job as if Me-Me wasn't standing there and demanding her full attention. But none of the people were leaving, even after they were bagged up and finished. It was as if they were ready for a fight. And Me-Me wanted so badly to give her sister a bullet in her head.

"Give me some money and I'll leave you alone." Micky said no again, and the lady that was being rung out just laughed. It was the last straw, and Me-Me picked up one of the cans closest to her and started to throw it at her. Her hand was grabbed, which smashed the can against her fingers. She was sure that her fingers were all broken.

"Put it down or I rip your arm off." It was the man from

earlier. And she'd bet her life on the fact that he would do just as he said he would. "Drop it or lose your ability to eat."

Dropping the can wasn't easy. She was in pain, and when she finally got her abused fingers to work and she let it go, the man squeezed her hand just a little harder and Me-Me cried out in pain.

"What the fuck is wrong with you? You broke my hand." He just crossed his arms over his chest and smiled at her, like a shark that had just eaten his prey. "Who the hell are you anyway, that you think you can come between my sister and I when we're having a conversation?"

"Her husband." Me-Me just shook her head and looked at Micky's hand. Sure enough, there was a large band and the biggest diamond she'd ever seen. "You harm her and that'll be it for you. You'll be dead."

"You can't say those things to me. There are witnesses here. I could have you arrested for this." He looked at the dozen or so people around her. Each and every one of them said that they'd seen nothing. "All I wanted was some money, and she refused me. How about you? Could you slip your new sister-in-law some much needed cash?"

"No." Me-Me was getting sick and tired of that word. "Leave now, or else you'll be in a cell right next to your sister. And if you want to take that as a threat, it's not. I promise you, if you don't leave here right now, you'll be arrested."

The police came into the store. None of them moved to take her, nor to assist her when she told them what this man had done to her. The man that seemed to be in charge of the law around here asked Lord Manning if he was all right.

"I am. And I thank you for your assistance. Ms. Patterson was just leaving."

She did but turned back to them all before she left. There

were so many things that she wanted to say, to do, but she wasn't going to be arrested either.

"You'll regret this. See if you don't, Micky. I want money. Either give it to me or I'll take it from you." Micky just smiled in her direction as she took the can off the belt and put it in the grocery bag like nothing was going on. "Damn it, you're not supposed to treat me like this. I'm your fucking sister."

"I'm only your sister when you want something. I'm finished with you." She then turned to the woman in front of her. "Mrs. Daniels, did you see that candy bars were on sale? I heard that your grandkids were coming for a visit."

Mrs. Daniels, or whatever her fucking name was, turned to a bin next to her and picked up a large handful of the sugary treats before she looked at her. Hatred seemed to ooze from her, like should she want it, burning fire would have come from her eyes and killed Me-Me where she stood.

Me-Me left. Not because she was frightened, but because she wanted to. She kept telling herself that over and over. It also blocked any thinking about what had just happened in there. Me-Me, for the first time in her life, was afraid of her little sister.

Chapter 6

After her sister left, Micky came to him. Holding her, he told Cooper what had happened. That was when he realized that Micky was crying. It was quiet, but he could feel her trembling as well.

"Go on ahead to my office, Lord Manning. I'll finish up out here." Delbert, the store manager, looked at the door where Mariam had gone and shook his head. "How did such a lovely girl come from the same gene pool as that one?"

"I've asked that same question daily. And I want to thank you for calling me when this started. I would hate to think what she'd have done to Micky if you hadn't." Delbert said that it had been his pleasure. "If you don't mind, I'd like to put a few more people in here when Micky is working. I don't want anything to happen to her."

"Of course, you don't. Yes, you go right ahead and do that for her."

Lucas moved to the office and closed the door behind them. As soon as the door clicked into place, Micky lost control of being able to hold back her sobbing and cried even harder.

KATHI S. BARTON

When she was able to lift her head to look at him, Lucas wanted to run out, shift into his dragon, and slay the beast for her. But he couldn't, he knew that. They didn't kill unless there was no other recourse for them. There were plenty ways to make this woman reap what she had sown, and he was going to enjoy watching them when it did happen.

"I'm a mess." He kissed her on the nose and told her she was still lovely to him. "Don't be an ass. I know what I look like when I cry. I'm all blotchy and my nose runs."

"There's my girl. If you want to know my opinion about what just happened out there, you stood up to a bully and came out on top." She glared at him and he had to laugh. "I can read minds. Did you know that? You might be able to do that as well, but you'll need instructions to do it. You could easily kill someone by raping their mind too aggressively." Lucas grinned at Micky. "I have to tell you that your sister has some evil shit going on. Also, I can make people believe whatever I want. She imagined that you were wearing a wedding ring, even though I didn't give you one yet. Sometimes the mind is so jumpy that I—"

"You read her mind?" Lucas told Micky that it was simple to do that, but he'd had a great deal of practice. "What is it you made her believe? She saw something that made her upset. Well, more upset."

Instead of answering her, Lucas got down on one knee and pulled out a cloth bag. It was beautifully made, what with the beads on it that made a dragon. Micky looked at him when he told her to open it.

"No, I don't think I want to. It's going to have something in it that is going to upset me. What is it?" Lucas laughed and told her to open it. "All right, I will. But if there is something bad in here, I'm going to go and live with one of your unmarried

82

brothers."

"It's not bad, and I'm not worried about that." Micky asked him why not. "Because each of them know that if they take you in, they'll be hurt. By me." He took the bag from her and dumped it in her palm.

"Oh, Lucas. It's beautiful." He had made it for her after going to the cave of riches they had and finding the perfect diamond. "Oh, look. It has our names in it too. Did you do this?"

"I did, and I'm glad that you like it. I told you it wasn't bad." He took the ring from her and kissed her hand. Sliding the ring up over her knuckle, he wasn't surprised when it fit her. "I love you with all that I am, Micky. You are my life's blood. Having you with me, it's hard to imagine a world without you standing beside me. I would love to marry you. Today. I have all the necessary paperwork filled out. All you need to do is say yes, and then you'll be my partner, my confidant, as well as the reason that I live. Will you marry me, Micky Mantle? Be my wife forever and ever?"

"Yes." He stood up and picked her up too. Lucas was just trying to figure out how to take her on the crowded desk when someone knocked on the door. "What is it?"

"I'm so very sorry, Lord Manning. But I am a little overwhelmed out here. Micky, do you think you can come out and help an old man?"

Lucas kissed Micky and patted her ass as she moved by him to go to the door. When she turned back, he could see worry on her face.

"I promise you, Micky, this will all be fine. It'll work itself out when the time is right."

When she nodded and left him there, Lucas sat on the edge of the desk. He was thinking of several things at once when he had to let his mind drift a bit. His chest got tight and he couldn't breathe well. Taking slow breaths, in and out, he felt the tension roll away. Carson spoke through their connection.

I'm telling you this, but I don't want you to say anything to Micky just yet. I found out that her great grandda was killed by Mariam Mantle. She poisoned him. He asked her how she knew. *I had his body exhumed yesterday. Pulled a few strings and told them that this was for you. Back me up if someone comes around. Anyway, she fed him a combination of arsenic and water hemlock. That one I had to look up, by the way. The coroner said that his body would have gotten that at the very end of his life. And it wouldn't have been an easy death for the man.*

No, I would think not. It doesn't take much to kill someone with it. Even animals aren't immune to the poison. It hits directly to the central nervous system and causes violent convulsions. After having a few grand mal seizures, death isn't that far behind. Lucas had suspected that one of them had knocked the old man off. Cain had been in reasonably good health until his sudden death. *What about her father?* She said that he was dead as well.

Died a happy man. Despite having cancer that he developed early in life, Peter was for all accounts very happy with his new wife and her children. The cancer was pretty aggressive. They gave him six months to live, but he only hung around for six days. Lucas wondered if Micky knew anything about her father's death and decided not to bring it up unless she did. *The reason that we know that Mariam did it is because she purchased the ingredients at the local herbalist in Columbus. She had to sign a waiver there because the owner of the place didn't want her coming back to her when someone was killed from it.*

And she remembers Mariam? Carson told him that she had one better. That the owner of the shop had cameras all over her store and kept them all. *I've had a look at it. She seemed almost giddy with what she was buying.*

She more than likely was. What else have you been able to find out? I'm sure that it's more than this. She told him that there was a great deal more. *Anything that will get me in trouble with my wife?*

You're marrying her? That's awesome. Congratulations on that. I know you are going to be so happy. Okay. It's not bad news, but you should know. He braced himself for the other shoe to drop. *Her grandda was a smart cookie. And he left everything to Micky. And your Micky is as clever as you when it comes to turning a little money into a great deal. Right now, she's worth just over six billion dollars, counting the three homes that she owns, two companies that she's on the board of directors of, as well as holding all the stocks on them. There is more, but you get the picture. And I don't think her sisters, or her mother, know just how much there really is. They were not present at the reading of the will. At least not from what I heard.*

Lucas sat there for several minutes after telling Carson thanks. She was wealthy. And working for minimum wage as a grocery store clerk. He was proud of her in that moment. Even though she didn't have to work, she did so. Standing up, he grinned. Her family was going to be in for a huge surprise if they pushed her too far. And he was looking forward to the shit hitting the fan.

The rest of his day was spent in his office. Alan kept checking on him, but Lucas was all right. He felt lighter than he had in a long time. And he was getting more done just by taking one thing at a time.

By the time Carson had sent over what she'd been able to unearth, he'd called his buddy in Washington D.C. Ronnie Chidlow told him what he'd been able to find out. And with what Grace had been able to find out with the help of Lincoln, things were falling into place to rid himself of his in-laws.

"I've been keeping an eye on your mother-in-law, Lucas. At least since she moved herself into the motel out on Thirty-

Three. She's into some major shit going on. We've got her, along with seven men, working on meth. They have a really nice set up there. Four rooms that have been converted into one. And Mariam is right there with them, helping them along to a prison cell forever." He asked what the holdup was. "There is someone that they work for. A private courier comes by once a week to drop off and pick up something. It's never the same guy nor the same day. They've shown up at midnight or thereabouts too. Hard to track them down. But as I said, they're working with someone we want to catch as well."

"And Mariam is working too?" Ronnie told him he thought she might be in charge of distribution. "How the hell did that come about?"

"Don't know, but I'm going to find out, that's for sure." He heard someone talking to him in his office. "I have to go, buddy. There are more bad guys wanting us to put them behind bars today."

After hanging up, Lucas sat there until someone snapped their fingers in front of his face. Smiling at Micky, he asked her how her day had gone.

"Pretty good, actually. Especially after Mariam the Second left. I was able to train one of the new hires on the computer. There really isn't much to it, just scan and go." She sat down on the chair by the empty fireplace. "I'm going to go and see Beth later tonight. She called me and asked that I come see her. I've already told her, on the phone, that I'm not bailing her out. But she asked that I come see her, and I will. It's not like she can physically hurt me not with her being behind bars."

"Do you want me to go with you? I can clear my calendar if you'd want." He wanted to be there for her. After the episode with Mariam the Second, he didn't want her to have to go through that once again. "It's no trouble whatsoever."

"I'll be all right. There aren't any cans she can toss at me. And with her behind those bars, I think the likelihood of her getting a gun or a knife is little to none. I'll be fine." He was going to have someone there. He wasn't going to let anything happen to her. "You are a worrywart. And weren't you supposed to stop stressing?"

"Yes, but I can't help myself. All I'll do is worry about them until this is a done deal." He told her what Ronnie had told him. "She's going down for a long time with this, Micky. This is her third strike, and they won't hold back on her prison sentence this time."

"I know. And I find myself not caring what happens to them. I've completely washed my hands of them. After today, I'm sure that I can cling to that no matter what happens from now on." He told her that he loved her. "And I love you. So very much."

~*~

Micky waited her turn to go and see her sister. She used that time to check on a few things that she had going, as well as how her employees were doing under the new ownership. She'd been talked into this deal, and now she was regretting it. Not because it was a bad investment, but it was taking up a lot of her time. Micky had to talk to Lucas when she got home. Telling him what the will of her great grandda had said would be the first thing she told him.

When her name was called, she sat at the round table. Other families were there as well. Very few of them looked like they were making it. She wondered what the families of men and women did when their sole support system was gone. Micky would have one of her lawyers check into that. When Beth sat in front of her, chained to the table like an animal, she was shocked at the way she looked.

"So, you came." Micky told Beth that was what she'd wanted. "Yes, so it is. I wanted to tell you something. But I first have to tell you something more. David was right to divorce me. And the fact that I won't be getting anything out of the marriage doesn't bother me as much as it did before. I've not been a good person for a very long time. If ever."

"Why?" Beth asked her what she meant. "Why did you want to tell me this, Beth? Because you're trying to make me feel sorry for you? It won't work. You have treated me like a monster since I was a child."

"You're right, I did that. And I didn't expect you to accept my apology to you. I don't deserve forgiveness. Not from you or anyone else that I had ties with. I'm the monster in all this. And I have no one to blame but myself for the tear in our relationship." Micky wasn't sure what to say to her, but Beth seemed to understand. "I think—and I'm not placing blame on her—but I think that a lot of my hatred to you came from Me-Me. You were never mean to us when we hurt you. You never retaliated when you could have. And all this time, from the very beginning, you did nothing to make our lives more difficult. Not once. And I'm sure that you could have."

"Yes. I have the means to do a great many things. But dealing with you and Mariam the Second isn't even a blip on the radar of things I have going on." Beth laughed and asked her if Me-Me knew that she called her the second. "Yes. She hates that as much as you hate being called Beth. I did it to get under her skin."

"I don't mind being called Beth. I never did, really. It was Me-Me who decided that I'd go by my first name and not the shortened one. She said that there couldn't be two short versions of our names, and she was the oldest." Beth looked around the room and back at her. "I believe that a lot of the things I did were because she told me to, and because she was the oldest. Like I said, I'm not blaming it all on her. I had free will. At any time, I could have stood up to her. But I was enjoying all the things I was getting into. To a point anyway."

"I don't know what to say to you about this." Beth nodded, as if she understood that she wouldn't. "Why are you doing this, Beth? Trying to make amends for what you and Mariam did to me. And to a lot of others."

"I was sick the other day. Nothing unusual for that. I'd been having belly issues for a few months. But I started throwing up blood, and they brought someone here. It didn't take him long to tell me what was happening to me. I have cancer. It's all over my body, and I only have a few months left to live." Micky said nothing. Beth seemed to understand that as well. "I've not told anyone, just you. There isn't much they can do for me now. It's too late. I was...I wasn't careful of things like getting myself checked out when I should, because I thought of myself as immortal. Or too young to die. Probably both."

"I'm sorry." Beth looked at her again. "When you get out of here, where will you go? There are places you can go and get care. I'll take care of the arrangements for you."

"Always so nice to people. It was another thing about you that Me-Me hated. No matter what, you never had a terrible thing to say to anyone. But I thank you for the care. I don't have anything. I didn't bring you here to give me anything either. Since I've been in here, I've had a lot of time to think. And I didn't much care for what I saw I'd become." For the first time in forever, Micky thought, she wanted to hug one of her sisters. "I'm being released the day after tomorrow. I've served my time here, and I'm going to have to wear a bracelet on my ankle. At least until my time is up. If you're sure that you'd like to help me out with some place to go and die, I'd really appreciate that.

I.... Micky, I don't want to die alone. I know that I have no right to ask this of you, and you have every right to tell me no. I'd be surprised if you didn't. Micky, please, forgive me enough to be there with me when I take my last breath. I beg of you."

"I'll be there for you, Beth. I will." She started thinking about arrangements and knew that she had to do one thing for her sister. "I want you to come to my home. You'll have good care, and I'll be with you when you need me. We can—I don't know, catch up on being sisters. I really have missed you."

They talked until their time was up. Micky told her that she'd be by tomorrow with her husband, and she could talk to him as well. Beth told her thanks at least a dozen times. It was the most difficult thing that she'd ever done, standing up to leave her there all alone. She looked over at the female guard that was watching over the room.

"I'd like to hug my sister. Please? She doesn't have much time left, and I need a hug from her. To feel her arms around me." The guard didn't look like she was going to say yes. Then she asked if she was Lord Lucas Manning's wife. "I am. He and I just married recently. But that doesn't allow me to hug Beth, does it?"

"He has been a good man since I've come here. There isn't any better than the Manning men. All right. But I'd like for you to hand me your purse, please. And both of you be careful of the other." Micky said that she would. "All right then. You go ahead. We all know that Mrs. Sharp doesn't have long to be here."

Beth grabbed her tightly. She was sobbing on her shoulder, telling her how much she loved her and wished things could have been different. Micky cried as well. They wouldn't have any time together, she and Beth. And she was sorry for that too. When they were finished, Micky held her for one more hug.

90

They'd lost so much time with this feuding, and she wanted to get as much as she could out of the time Beth had left.

Before leaving the jail, Micky told Beth that she'd be back tomorrow. When she was driving down the road to home, she had to suddenly pull over. The tears were making it hard for her to see, and her heart was broken—not for herself, but for her sisters. Both of them had done so much to her, and now one of them was going to die. And Micky was so sorry for that and it hurt her badly to think of the suffering Beth would have to go through now.

You all right? She told Lucas that she was and told him what she'd found out. Also, what she wanted to do. *Yes, that's a good idea. Bring her here, and I'll have a medical staff on duty for her. Whatever she needs, we'll do it for her.*

Micky cried harder. All her life she'd been looking for someone to love her, and he'd found her. She didn't normally have any faith in the fates, didn't understand soulmates. And in one chance meeting, she'd found it all in the man who loved her dearly.

The rest of the ride home was uneventful. She would have bursts of tears once in a while, but not like she had when she'd had to pull over. Beth was dying—soon. The guard had told her when she asked as she was leaving that it had taken all Beth had to sit with Micky today. And that she wouldn't make it much longer.

Lucas was waiting for her when she pulled into the drive. He didn't say anything, but kissed her gently on the mouth, then took her hand. She had no idea what they were going to do when they got to the backyard, but she was much too fragile to care right now. He sat her on a chair that had been moved to the largest part of the yard.

"Come fly with me." Micky frowned at him, not really sure

91

what he meant. She couldn't fly, could she? "No. But I can. I have yet to show you my dragon. I thought that I'd show him to you and then take you on a trip."

"You mean that I can fly beside you?" He smiled and shook his head while he backed up. "Lucas, I'm not so sure about this. What if you drop me or I slip through...what would you carry me in anyway?"

"My heart." When he was perhaps fifteen or so feet from her, Micky felt the tightening of the air around her. Even the ground seemed to push her up a bit. But when he stood before her as his dragon, Micky stood up. *I shall never hurt you in any way.*

"You're beautiful. I never thought that something so large could be so lovely. Can I touch you?" The big dragon laid his head down on the ground as it moved to accommodate her.

Micky was keenly aware of his size—the sharpness of his teeth and the way his scales seemed to be as large as she was. Putting out her hand, she cut her finger on the spike that she'd not noticed at the end of the blue colored scale.

Let him have a taste of you through the wound, Micky. He'd love that very much. Putting out her trembling hand, she felt the heat of the dragon's breath when he opened his mouth. And when his tongue slid out from his teeth, all she could think about was that she could fit whole in his mouth and never touch the sides. *He'd never harm you either, Micky. He's here for your protection and for mine.*

Micky thought that he was going to lick the wound, but Lucas told her to put her injured finger onto his tongue so that he might taste her that way. With trembling hands, she did as he asked, and felt his power dance over her skin, her mind, as well as her sight. It was as if she had been renewed somehow, that all her troubles had been washed away in that single moment of time.

When he sat up on his hind legs, she watched as he curled his tail around his massive body. Touching him wherever she could reach, she noticed the difference in his scales according to where they were. The ones on his chest, gleaming white in the evening dusk, were harder, like armor she supposed. When she was able to touch those on his tail, they were harder still than the ones on his chest. While she was running her hand over the long steel-like scales he asked her to back up, and when she did, his entire body became deadly.

There were long sharp barbs on his chest and his tail. His head was covered in a thick shell-like thing that covered all but his mouth. There were eye holes in it so that he could see, she imagined. His arms and legs were covered in the same spiked shell.

This is my battle dress. She told Lucas that she could see that. *I can slay large groups of those that try and kill us this way with just a movement of my tail. My chest plate is heavier, and also covered in deadly poison that would slay a man or foe immediately.*

"Why didn't it hurt me? When I cut myself on your scale?" He uncurled his hand from his body. The nails, she supposed they might be called, were as long as she was tall, and twice as wide. Climbing into his palm, she sat down and looked at him when he raised her up to eye level. "If you drop me, you can be sure that I'll make you pay bigtime. Understand?"

Yes, my lady. And as to why you weren't hurt, it is because you are my other half, my mate. And my dragon knows not to harm you.

They were in the sky in moments. Looking out between his fingers, she could see the world below them. The span of his wings was as marvelous as anything that she'd ever experienced before. When she saw other dragons join them, Micky knew that it was the other Mannings, out for a lovely ride in the darkening skies.

Standing up, knowing that she was safe in his care, she looked at the sky from a position that she'd never seen before. The clouds were so fluffy that she could imagine herself walking on them. The wind in her face, blowing her hair back, was clean smelling, as if it had never been touched by either the pollution or pollens from the ground. Laughing, enjoying her ride so much, she told Lucas that she loved him with all her heart.

And I you, my lady. You are everything that I could have hoped for and more in having a mate. She soared through the air with her dragon, and knew that for as long she lived, this ride, the first of many she hoped, would be the most precious of them all.

Chapter 7

They were all on pins and needles today. Well, she was anyway. And Mariam was going to make sure that the big boss was going to take notice of her. She needed to have someone take care of her. Straightening up her clothing for the tenth time in as many moments, Mariam decided that she'd never looked better.

Working in the lab for the last week had weighed heavily on her body. She wasn't getting enough sleep for one thing, and the thought of what she was going to buy with all her money was keeping her up at nights too. So far, in a short week she had earned nearly ten grand. Giddy with the prospect of having someone as rich as the boss taking her under his wing, she was convinced that she was going to set her up for life. Her two daughters, Me-Me and Bethany, would benefit from this as well.

"My baby girls are going to be so surprised when they find out what I've done." Laughing out loud, she danced a little jig and had to keep herself from laughing too much. "You don't want to be locked away at this point, now do you, Mariam?"

No, she didn't. For a brief moment she thought of Micky, wondering, she supposed—as any mother would—what her baby was up to. Not that she'd help her out if she was down on her luck. Micky had burned that bridge a long time ago. But she would like to see her once more, after she was settled in her new home, to rub it in her face that she'd done so well for herself.

Going next door to hang out with her boss, she wondered what he thought of her dress. Before she could ask, they heard someone pulling into the stone driveway that also was used for a parking lot. Mariam hadn't been this nervous in a very long time.

"You have my product?" The man didn't even look in her direction, but at her boss. As always, no names were given, nor did anyone seem to care. She did—she wanted this man to take her in. "I've been behind the last few days. I'm glad that you were able to step up your game and get me more."

"It was my pleasure. We have it all ready for you. As well as an extra ten percent for goodwill. We want to do business with you now, and into the future if possible." Gone was the hick accent that he used. There was a deepness to his voice that hadn't been there before. Now it was more authoritative, more refined.

"Good. Good. Now, let me try it out. I have me a man here—he'll do the testing. I surely hope this is the real deal. I'd hate to have to bring in a second crew to take care of you all." He glanced at her then back at her boss. "You getting some on the side here? She looks a little old for you, don't you think?"

"What the hell is that supposed to mean? I've been working with him for several days now. And I am not old." She wanted to punch the man in the head, but all he did was laugh. At her. "You might want to think about the fact that I'm a valuable part of your business right now instead of pissing me off."

"Little lady, I'm the type of man that doesn't care how much I piss people off. In fact, you keep working your way into my being in a bad mood and you might find yourself deep in a hole with a bullet between your eyes." He looked at her boss. "Get rid of her as soon as possible."

"I'm not leaving here." He turned to her, his gun out and pointed at her. "Listen, I think we got off on the wrong foot here. I was hoping that you'd, you know, find me pretty enough to have me hanging on your arm. You know, be my sugar daddy."

She smiled at him, a smile that she had practiced for days when she was younger. It said, I'm smart and I can make you so happy. Sultry, she thought it was called. But sexy was what she was going for this time.

The man laughed then. It started out as a little burst of it. Then he was nearly falling over with it before she began to see red. This wasn't the way to treat a woman, and she slapped him across the face. She knew her mistake the moment that she did it.

"Get rid of her any way that you want but I want her gone today." Her boss nodded and said that he'd gladly take care of it. "Good. Now, let's see what we have here."

Mariam was held by one of the men that had been sitting beside her the entire time she'd been working here. He restrained her in a way that hurt her shoulders, and with his beefy hands holding her like he was, she was sure to have a bruise when he let her go. After struggling for several minutes, she gave up to watch what was going on now. The fuckers could not put her out when she'd been working so hard.

A metal case was brought in. It reminded her of the kind that Cain, her ex-husband's grandfather, had carried around when he was out and about. She'd never known what was in it, and neither had her husband. The fucker probably carried around all his money like that, so he'd not have to stoop to having too little cash when he needed it.

The case was opened and turned toward her boss. There were neat stacks of hundred-dollar bills—she could count eight just on the top. And she'd bet anything that those had three or four stacks under them. Christ almighty, there had to be over a million dollars there. And it was untraceable cash. Mariam was sorry now that she'd spouted off to the man. He was obviously wealthier than anyone she'd ever met.

The money was put in the large safe that had been brought in just yesterday. It was massive, and she wondered now if it was going to hold all the money that was brought in this way. She could have so much fun finding ways to spend it. And her girls, the ones that she cared about, they'd be so happy that she'd done this for them. Because Mariam was going to take it and run as soon as possible.

She was just working out the plan when her boss came back to her. The big boss, he'd gone out to his car and appeared to be leaving. Mariam was told to kneel down on the floor, right now. She had no idea what was going on, but if this guy wanted a blow job from her, that she'd almost be willing to do it. But the floor?

"I most certainly will not get on this floor. Have you seen the filth that's there?" She struggled again when she was shoved to a kneeling position by the man behind her. "You have to realize that I'm not going to be as comfortable giving you what you want. Not with me being afraid of the germs here."

"What is it you think I want? You to suck me off? No thanks. I wouldn't touch you with a ten-foot pole. Never. You are just too—I was going to say gross, but it would be like having my mom do it. And honey, you are so not my type, even if I wasn't gay."

He put a gun to her forehead and it felt like he was trying to ram it in her head he was pushing it so hard. It hit her then — they were talking about taking care of her by killing her off. Mariam looked up at the man about to shoot her as all hell broke loose in the rooms.

There were men in vests, people with helmets on their heads. And all of them were shouting at them to put their hands over their heads and kneel down, their guns pointed at everyone in the room. She was let go then and had started to rise when she was told to get back down.

"Look. I have nothing to do with these people. I've had enough insults from them to last me a long time. If you don't mind I'm going to — "

"Lady, get the fuck down on the floor or I'll blow your fucking head off." She thought the man was very rude. "Lady, if you run, I'm going to hurt you. I will be justified by you trying to escape being arrested."

"Well of course I'm going to run."

Mariam only made it to the sidewalk when suddenly she was hit in the back of the head. Whatever it had been, Mariam saw stars before she completely blacked out.

Waking up, she realized that she was in the hospital. There was a white curtain around her, and she started to sit up when she discovered she couldn't move her hands. Looking down at her right hand, she saw that it was cuffed to the bed. So was her right ankle. Glancing around the small space, she saw a man with his rifle, or whatever it was called, across his chest like he was just waiting for her to try something. Also, he was staring at her.

"What happened?" He didn't speak, not even to say he hoped she was all right or anything. "I asked you what happened. And why am I cuffed like a criminal, like an animal?"

Her head was pounding—she was nearly sick from it. Lying back down, the curtain around her was tossed back. The man in the suit had a badge hanging around his neck like a set of pearls that she once had. Mariam saw that it said DEA, Drug Enforcement Administration. She asked him the same questions that she had the dick beside her.

"As for what happened, you resisted arrest and had to be made aware of who was in charge at that moment. When you were unconscious, we were able to subdue you quite easily. You should have stayed where you were instead of standing when you had just been told, at gunpoint I might add, to kneel down." He pulled out some paperwork from inside his jacket. "I can tell you, for now, we have you on a list of charges including drug trafficking, drug paraphernalia, sale of drugs, and—"

"Hold on there, buster. I did nothing of the sort. I don't have any idea what you're talking about." He sat down, and she felt her skin itch, like he could see right inside of her head. "I was working for that man, but I didn't sell any of it, nor did I give any of it away. That would have gotten me— That guy that was there, he was going to shoot me in the head. He was told to get rid of me, and I thought that they meant they were going to fire me. Whoever he is, he was going to kill me."

"Yes, we knew that. But we weren't there to save you. We had bigger targets to take care of." She asked him when she was getting cut loose. "You're not, Ms. Mantle. You are here for the long haul this time. You might have been able to get a bond if there were not such harsh circumstances. And if you hadn't tried to run. But we both know that you don't have the money for that anyway. Also, and this one just tickles me to no end, you're going to be tried separately for the murder of Cain Mantle, the grandfather of your husband. He was a good man, and you killed him."

"I did no such thing." But she had, and it hadn't done her any good either. "He was an old man, a cantankerous one, and died in his sleep."

"That's what everyone was led to believe. But just recently his body was exhumed, and tests were done. He had been poisoned with a mixture of water hemlock and arsenic. We have a video of you buying the poisons; plus, we found them in the garage of your former home. Hiding it behind the wallboard was good, but when you have someone telling exactly where it was, it makes things perfect. What do you have to say for yourself?" Mariam didn't have any idea what to say to him. "Your daughter was kind enough to tell us where to look, as well as how you rushed into having him buried. Beth has been working hand in hand with us for a few days now."

"You lie. My daughter would never do that to me. And her name is Bethany, not that horrid name Beth. Me-Me, my other daughter, picked out her nickname. God only knows why she went with that." She needed time to think. To plan. Mariam thought that she could plan and execute herself out of this mess. "My head is hurting from that brute who hit me. There was no cause for acting so violent towards me. As I told him, I have no idea what you are talking about."

He stood up and she jerked on her cuff, hoping that he'd get the idea that she wanted him to undo her restraints. There wasn't any way that she was going to get out of here and run if he didn't. And he didn't, leaving her in the curtained off area with her guard.

Mother fuck, she was so screwed right now. And she'd bet anything that the fuckers had taken all her hard-earned cash while they were at it. She'd have to remember to ask for it when they came back. Maybe it would be enough to get her out on bond.

~*~

Lucas was just finishing up his day when Tristan came into his office. Not only was it unusual for him to come downtown, but he never entered a room that wasn't his own without knocking.

"Are you all right?" Tristan looked at him; his eyes were sort of glazed over, and Lucas didn't think he was hearing him. "Tristan, are you all right? Did something happen?"

"I'm afraid." He asked him what he was afraid of. "Life. We aren't going to die. None of us are, and I'm bored with it."

"Bored with life, you mean." Tristan nodded and leaned back in his chair. "What is it you have in mind to do? See the world? I believe, overall, it's changed a great deal since we were anywhere. Do you wish to take up a hobby? You have to tell me what it is you want to do about this. Short of having you put to a permanent sleep, I'll help you anyway that I can."

"No. I don't want that. I'd miss you. I mean—you know what, I have no idea. But it occurred to me when I went to see Cooper this morning that I don't have any involvement in the things around me. Even the wives, including yours, have a job to do. I don't contribute to anything to keep me occupied." Lucas knew what he meant about that too. A few decades ago, he was right where his brother was. "You have anything, and I mean anything, that I can do?"

"I do, as a matter of fact. And I think you're going to enjoy it too. The high school is short staffed this year. They need not only a history teacher—and you have to admit, we'd be perfect for teaching that—but also an assistant coach for the boys' athletics department. Such as seasonal sports."

He could see that Tristan's interest was there. Lucas handed him the application that he himself had planned on filling out. As soon as he had it in his hands, Tristan began filling it out. This was just what he needed. And he'd be helping the community as well.

"It says here that I'll be paid for the games out of the booster funds for each sport. Do you know if there is a way to have it go right back to them? They need it a great deal more than I do." Lucas told him what his plan would have been, not mentioning that he himself had thought of that as well. "Yes, I can see that working out better. I know that we support the school anyway, so I can just donate it back in the form of a gift to the teachers. I'm sure that they could use it in the last few months of school when all their supplies start to run low."

When he was finished, having had Lucas type up a resume that he could use, Tristan left. He said he was going to go to the school now and find out if he could do the job. Lucas made two calls, making sure that they understood that Tristan was just as educated as he was and would do them a world of good. He also mentioned not to tell him that Lucas had planned to take the job.

As the evening wore on, Lucas thought of a few more things that he could take care of now. That way he'd be able to sleep in and wake up Micky in the most wonderful way. The thought of her and how responsive she was to just a simple touch made his cock hard and full. Smiling, waiting for a response to one of his emails, he thought of everything he was going to do to his pretty wife.

When his phone rang he was startled by the sound, deep into his plans for Micky.

"Lord Manning? This is FBI agent Lance Caldwell. I have some good news for you, and some not so good. We've arrested Mariam Mantle. Word is you married her daughter recently." He told him that he had. "I don't believe that your wife is involved, but we'd like to question her. Just to clear up her name. A formality, if you please."

"I'll talk to her. I don't know if you're aware of this or not, but Micky broke ties with her family years ago. She had, however, made peace with one of them. Beth is currently living out her last days at our home. She doesn't have long to live, I'm sorry to say." Agent Caldwell said that he'd heard that as well. And Beth had helped them a great deal before leaving the hospital. "I'm happy that she could do that for you. I think that she's burning her bridges, so to speak, on the other two, her mom and Mariam the Second, as my wife calls her."

"She's a piece of work, the mother is. If you don't mind me saying so, it's about time she got herself caught. This will close a great deal of trouble that she's caused over the years." Micky came into his office, talking to Alan about something, and he interrupted Agent Caldwell to tell him that Micky was here now, and asked if he could have a moment to bring her up to speed. "Yes, yes, you go right ahead. I'll hold."

Lucas told her everything that the agent had said. When she told him that she didn't know anything about her mother, Lucas explained that he didn't think she would. But he still wanted to cross all his t's and dot all the i's in this.

"All right. If this will seal the lid on her going to prison, I'm all for it." She sat down on his lap and took the call. He could hear the questions that Caldwell asked, as well as Micky's answers. They made plans for her to come to the jail to get everything recorded. "I'll be there. But I want my husband there as well. He's a good attorney, and I don't want anything to come back and bite me in the ass. As I'm sure you can understand."

"Oh yes, I do understand. And I was going to suggest that you bring your attorney. I don't anticipate anything coming of your interview. But as I told Lord Manning, we don't want her getting out again on something we didn't do." Micky told him that was fine. "If you could spare a couple of hours, I'd really appreciate it."

"You'll have to come here, I'm afraid. My sister, Beth, she doesn't have long to live, and I'm trying to spend every moment with her that she has left. Which, the doctors say isn't long." He told her he was sorry. Lucas could hear the compassion in his voice even over the phone.

When she disconnected the call after making arrangements for him to come to their house, Micky got up and moved around the room. His heart broke for her. Beth really had very little time left.

"The doctor just left. He said that the move from the jail to here took its toll on her. But he told me that she was resting better here, and she seems to have come to terms with her impending death. She has, but I haven't." He knew that as well. "She...we both waited too long to make this work for us. I know that this is only because she's at the end of her time, but I'm so sorry that it took this for her to come to me."

"I agree with you on that. All that came between the two of you, for the most part, was Mariam and your mother. They bullied Beth into just about anything, I'm to understand. And you were hurt by it most of all." Micky came to sit on his lap again. "You are going to be all right, love. You're stronger than both of them together. And your mother, being in jail, cannot hurt you anymore."

"I think I want to go and see her. Not today, but soon. Agent Caldwell is coming by to talk to me. I was thinking that I'd go there and see what she has to say for herself. I'm betting that they'll have Mariam the Second soon too."

Lucas had some more news for Micky, but he thought it could wait until later. He knew where Mariam the Second was, and that she was going to be arrested soon. The two of them, both Mariams, would be in jail before nightfall. And Lucas was so happy about it that he wondered what sort of celebration Micky would like to have. There was so much that he could do for her, he just couldn't decide on one.

Lucas was finished for the evening, having gotten all the work done for tomorrow as well. Having someone helping him, a staff that Alan had hired, he was less stressed as well as sleeping much better. Smiling, he thought that part could be attributed to all the sex he was having. But whatever it was, he was thrilled to no end about it.

Going into the living room, he was disappointed to find the room empty. But as he was going to the stairs to find Micky, he heard her. Something had happened, and taking the stairs two at a time, he held her while the nurse stood over the bed, feeling for the pulse of Beth. Lucas knew she was at peace now. And she'd not died alone, her biggest fear.

"Can you call Agent Caldwell for me please? Explain to him why I can't do this today." He told her he'd do that. And while he was holding her in his arm as she sobbed, he let the rest of his family know that Beth Mantle Sharp had passed away in her rest.

Do you think Micky could stand some company? We'd all like to be there for her right now. Lucas thanked Lincoln and told him that he thought she could use it. *Good. We'll stay until she kicks us to the curb. Give her our love, will you? This hurts me so badly that she's going through this.*

Whenever anyone died around them—and over the years, there had been a great many of them—he'd think of his own father and hurt for the loss of him. Holding onto Micky while the nurse made the necessary calls, he wondered if Beth had hung on to be with Micky and believed that to be true. No one, he thought, wanted to die alone. Or in this case, unloved.

Chapter 8

Me-Me was contemplating whether or not she could cook a pork chop on the little grill that she'd swiped from someone's backyard a couple of nights ago. So far, all she'd used it for was boiling water, which she wasn't good at either. Putting it back, she moved to the ground hamburger. She was sure that she could manage cooking that by herself.

Having been on her own as long as she had, Me-Me decided that she hated her own company. She knew that there were people out there that loved the quiet and the peace, but not her. She needed action and sounds. Music if she could manage it, but something other than her own breath coming out of her sour tasting mouth. She made her way to the toothpaste and brush part of the littlest grocery store she'd ever been in. They didn't even have an olive bar, nor a place to buy fresh bread.

After pocketing a travel size toothbrush and paste, she moved to the instant food section. This was about all she could manage. There were good instructions, and she could actually follow them. Me-Me couldn't believe how difficult it was just to make a sandwich.

There was bread and meat. Lettuce and tomato had to be cut up and cleaned. And she wasn't going to go there about mustard or mayo. There were so many varieties of them, she had to just take three or four of them just to figure out what brand she liked. No, cooking and all the stuff that went with it could just stay in the kitchen where it belonged.

Me-Me had decided not to kill her sister. Micky could go on being whatever she wanted to be so long as she paid her once a month. Figuring out how much she wanted was difficult. Since Me-Me had never cared about the price of things that she bought nor how they were paid for once she put them on the card, she wasn't sure what to demand.

Pocketing a few more items that she wanted, she made her way around the store. There were so many things that she wanted from here. A nice wine would have been wonderful, but they only sold bottles that were shiny and bright. Again, not knowing the cost of things, she still thought the prices were too low for her to enjoy them.

After getting as much as she could carry back to the house she was staying in, Me-Me made her way to the front to leave. These people were so stupid, and it was small wonder they were constantly having sales in the place. She'd been coming here for the last three days and had never been caught.

Grabbing one more item, Me-Me took the bottles of water and stuck them in her bag. She was going to have to get herself something larger if she was going to have to do this for much longer. Perhaps she'd buy herself a nice huge bag when Micky paid her some of her money. Whatever she had, it couldn't be very much, but Me-Me was going to demand at least half of it. That was the least she could do for her eldest sister.

Walking out into the sunlight blinded her for a moment. She'd been in the store for a long time, and the place didn't have a single window in it. How was a person supposed to know the weather before they got up to the front? Me-Me would have designed it much differently.

A man grabbed her arm and she came around swinging. Of course, her arm got tangled up in her bag, so she wasn't able to hit him all that hard. Me-Me suddenly found herself on the ground with her arms pulled painfully up behind her back.

"What is the meaning of this? Unhand me right this minute!"

But he didn't, and she heard her shoulder pop. Christ, it hurt, and she started screaming about suing them and making them pay for hurting her so badly. When she was helped to stand up, she looked at the police officers that were in front of her. Whatever was going on, she was in deep shit. They were armed in vests, guns out, and a big fucking dark van with SWAT on the side of it.

"What do you think you're doing?" The cop in front of her took her purse off her shoulder. "That is private property. Hand that back to me this second. I can't believe that you're accosting someone coming out of the store. There isn't that much in there anyway."

Her bag was dumped on the concrete in front of her. It was all there, all the evidence that they needed to arrest her. And when she was asked if she had a receipt, she refused to answer the man. But she did ask to talk to her sister.

"When you're booked, we'll let you make your phone call. Until then, I'm going to read you your rights." And he did that, asking her at the end if she understood what was being said to her.

"No, I don't know what you're talking about. I paid for everything in that bag. You have no way of proving anything anyway." He was handed a small reader like thing and turned

111

it toward her. There she was, putting things in her bag and the pockets of her clothing. Before she could ask if they could prove it was her, she looked right up at the camera as if saying hello to someone. Christ, she was as stupid as they came. "I want a lawyer."

He just laughed but told her that she had a right to one. Then they shoved her, quite literally, into the back of a large van and she was buckled into the seat. There was no one else in there with her. She thought they must have had fun arresting someone for simply trying to have a meal. She wondered what Bethany would say when she called her for help.

Bethany had been released from jail three days ago. She was both surprised by it and pissed off. Why hadn't she at least tried to get in touch with her? Or better yet, let her know so that she could bunk up with her for a few days. None of this would have happened if she'd just done that one simple thing.

As soon as they were at the jail, she was taken inside and booked. Up until now she'd thought that it only meant getting your picture taken and someone making you take a shower naked, so they could throw some kind of powder on you. Me-Me didn't actually think that they threw powder on you in a jail, but this was unknown to her. She wished she'd have asked her sister about it.

The booking, or whatever it was that they did to her, only took about an hour. But for some reason, she thought they were just dragging it out to be mean. Why did they need her fingerprints? A side view of her face? And why did she have to put on this orange thing when she wasn't going to be there that long?

"I'd like to call my sister." The man told her that she'd have to wait. "No, I know my rights. I need to call her, so she can come down here and bail me out. She'll do it too, because we're sisters."

No one cooperated with her on the call. She was taken down the long brightly lit hallway and put in a cell. It took her several minutes to figure out that the person in the cell across from her was her mother. Calling out for her got her shouted at, but her mom stood up and came to the bars that separated them.

"What happened to you? And where the hell have you been? I was looking for you, Mother." She told her that she'd been falsely arrested on drug charges. "They caught me shoplifting. Or so they're trying to pin on me. I need to find Bethany. I heard that she was released a few days ago. I don't suppose you have her number, do you?"

"No. When she was tossed out on her ass, I didn't get the chance to see if she was able to get herself a phone. Ex-husbands take that away from you too when they throw you to the curb. What about your husband? Can you call Neil?" She told her what he'd done to her. "Christ, that's not right. Just to get you when you're down. I'm beginning to think that all men are shitheads, and there isn't one out there worth shit."

Me-Me thought of Micky's husband. For whatever reason, she didn't think he'd do anything to hurt Micky. He looked at her like she was as fragile as glass and as beautiful as a newly blossomed rose. She had read that somewhere and thought that it was absolutely perfect for the way the two of them looked at each other.

"Did you know that Micky was living with some guy?" Me-Me told her mom that Micky was married to him. "You don't say. Well, I can bet that won't last very long. She's an idiot. And a thief. To think that she wouldn't share the money that she got from old Cain. And by the way, they're blaming me for his death. They told me that Bethany told them where to find the stuff that I used to knock the old buzzard off. Christ, I

hated that man. Forever in our business. And he adored Micky.
The fucking bastard."

Me-Me thought of her involvement in the death of Micky's
first fiancé. She'd murdered him in much the same way as she
had an ex-husband of hers several years ago. She had waited
until he was asleep, then gone in and put a rope around his
neck. The problem that she'd run into with Richard was that
he was much younger than her ex, and a good deal stronger.
Me-Me had strained her back and her arms when she'd finally
gotten him tied up and hung him from the beam in the room.
Christ, she wished that she'd have asked him to pretend to
hang himself before she killed him. It would have been much
lighter work for her.

When someone came to the cells with a tray for both of
them, Me-Me wanted to scream at the woman who had it that
she wasn't a criminal and she would not be treated as one. Her
mother, however, moved to the back of her cell and received
her tray of food.

"Either do it my way, Ms. Patterson, or you can starve
tonight. Breakfast isn't until eight in the morning, and that's
a good fourteen hours from now." She moved back but she
didn't like it. She'd missed lunch as well as breakfast today
because she hadn't hidden away her food good enough and
some animals got into it. "Good girl. Now, you keep behaving
yourself and we won't have to hold your meals or any calls that
you might have. By the way, your sister has heard that you've
been arrested and she's coming to see you."

"Will she have bail money too? Did you ask her?" The
woman cop told her that she'd not. It wouldn't have mattered
anyway—there hadn't been one set yet, and she'd have to wait
on that. "Who do I have to blow to get this thing rushed? I don't
want to be in here anymore than my mother."

The officer just walked out, laughing the entire way. Me-Me wanted to toss her food at the woman, but it smelled so good that she decided that she'd do it next time. Sitting down on the only piece of furniture in the room, Me-Me pulled the cover off her meal and stared at it. Christ, this was how they fed a person in jail? If so, she might want to stay here forever.

There was thinly sliced roasted turkey over a slice of white bread. Mashed potatoes that were still steaming, and the gravy was as creamy looking as the potatoes. There was a serving of green beans in a good-sized bowl, carrots swimming in butter and brown sugar. Under the other cover was a large slice of lemon meringue pie, with the meringue so tall on the filling she thought that she could gladly make a meal of it.

There were warm biscuits with butter on the side, cups of both tea and milk, as well as a cup of hot coffee. Me-Me asked her mom if she had eaten like this since she'd been there.

"Yes. This morning for breakfast, I had three scrambled eggs. Real eggs, not those ones from a carton. There was English muffins, bacon and ham, as well as some gravy — sausage gravy that I poured all over the biscuits that had come with it." Her mom laughed. "I missed my lunch, I had to go and talk to my attorney. I can't afford one, so they're paying for that too. I could do worse, I guess. They're trying to get me on killing off Cain, in addition to drug charges. What are you in for again?"

"Shoplifting. I tried to get out of that, but they have me on video. I tell you, Mom, there just aren't enough trusting people around anymore. I mean, years ago, when we were all living together, you didn't have to worry about cameras and such." Her mom agreed with her.

She ate the rest of her meal in silence. The meal was as good as if not better than it smelled, and she made a pig of herself by eating every last bit of it, even running the last part of her biscuit in the gravy so as not to miss a single bite.

When they came to get their trays, she did as she was told this time. Me-Me wasn't going to miss a single meal. She didn't know the next time she'd have one. As soon as Bethany was able to bail her out, she'd be bunking with her for a bit. And Bethany couldn't cook any better than she could.

There was a click-click noise coming down the hall about an hour later. Me-Me had been dozing when she heard it and got up to see who it was. She was hoping it was Bethany — she needed someone to tell her things were going to be just fine.

"Hello Mother, Mariam the Second. How do you like jail life? I'm sure that you're going to be spending a good long time here. Which is good. I want both of you to rot in hell for what you've done to me."

"I don't want you here. Where is Bethany? She's been avoiding me. Tell her to come down here with some money so she can get me out of here." Micky told her no. "You will do it, Micky, or so help me, when I do get out of here, you're going to regret it."

"Beth died two days ago. She had been diagnosed with cancer while in jail. By then it was too late — it had spread throughout her body." Me-Me told her she was lying. "No. I'd never lie to you about this. She was buried this morning. I've only come here to let you know."

"You bitch. You killed her, didn't you? I'll get you for this. Just as soon as you pay my bond. You're going to pay, Micky." Me-Me was afraid that she wasn't lying. Bethany was dead? It was something that she'd have to check on.

As she walked away, Me-Me shouted to her to come back, to tell the truth. But it did her little to no good. Micky walked out. And she was sure that would be the last time she saw her sister.

116

~*~

Lucas didn't know what to think when Micky came out of the cell area and went straight outside. He'd come with her, but she wanted to do this all on her own. Following her out, he was careful not to ask any questions. She'd tell him when she was ready.

When he started the truck up, he made his way to the dealership. They were going to pick out a car for Micky. While he did have a few other vehicles, she couldn't drive a stick shift. Pulling into the big parking lot, she finally looked at him.

"I know that you and I can't have a baby of our own. I understand why. But I'd like a child with you. To raise to be someone we can be proud of." He told her that they could do that at any time. "All right. We can do that. I know that it's a little difficult when they're checking you out, but I'm sure that we'll be able to handle it. I told them that Beth had passed away and what had happened." Lucas waited. "They didn't ask where she was buried or if she had a nice funeral. Neither of them asked if she'd been in a great deal of pain. All Mariam the Second could do was shout at me about paying her bond. And get this—she wanted me to pay it so that she could get out and harm me."

"I'm sorry, love. I really am. They sound like very selfish people." She told him that they were. "Would you like to go home? We can do this some other time."

"No. I want to buy a car today. I want to pretend that everything is normal, for a little while, anyway." She looked at him then. "You're the best husband a woman could ask for. You're kind, loving, and you're great in bed. But mostly, you love me."

"I do. Forever." They got out of his truck and started looking at cars. Micky knew what she wanted, and they were

117

still hunting for it when the salesperson came up to them. Lucas told him, "I think we're doing all right. We're looking."

"Why don't we go and see what you qualify for, and that'll narrow down your search for you." He'd started to ask Lucas, the man, what he wanted when Micky took over.

"Are you saying that it doesn't look like we can afford a certain price range? Or are you trying your best to see if we not only qualify for one, but you can add on some extras to pad your commission?" He sputtered and turned red. And Lucas knew that was just what the man was going to do. "When we're ready to talk to someone about what we want, we'll come to them. My husband told you that we were looking. Now go away."

The man practically ran away from them. Lucas was laughing as he pulled Micky into his arms. She was crying, just a little, so he held her until she was ready to talk to him. It had been a hard day on all of them.

"I was so rude to that man." Lucas told her that she'd been right, he did want to up his commission. "But I had no reason to treat him that way. I guess I'm a little more stressed than I thought."

"You did what needed to be done. I don't like to be shadowed when I know what I want either. Maybe you can tell me what it is you're looking for and we can get it." She smiled at him. "I'm thinking you want something fast and red."

"I did at one time, but not anymore. If you were serious about us having a child, I'm going to need something practical. It might have to be red, but I want four doors and a little bit more space in the back for presents." When she wiggled her brows at him, he laughed. And it made her laugh. As they searched the lot, the salesman came to them again.

"I'm so sorry, Lord Manning. I just wanted to tell you that.

I am very sorry, and I thank your wife for putting me in my place. I was pushy, and I need to not be." He started to go away again when Micky called him back. "I'm sorry to you as well, my lady."

"I was rude as well. And I am profoundly sorry for taking my horrible day out on you. If you'd be so kind—what is your name?" He told her. "Hello, Dan. I'm looking for something that can hold at least four, but I'd prefer that six people could sit in it comfortably. I haven't driven in the snow here, but I'm to understand that it can be brutal."

"Oh yes. And as soon as it does snow, I'd suggest that Lord Manning take you to a large parking area and practice in it. I'd not want anything to happen to either of you." Lucas could tell that the man was trying very hard not to over sell them, or to insult them again. "I do have something that you might want. It's just come in. The only thing, it's red. I don't know if you're aware of this or not, but red cars seem to get pulled over more than any other."

"Let's go see it. And for the record, I wanted a red car anyway."

They walked among the cars that all had tags on them and entered the showroom. But they didn't stop there. Dan took them to the big open garage where employees were unloading cars. And Lucas saw the car before Micky did.

Micky squealed with delight at the SUV. It had three row seating, just like she wanted. Four-wheel drive, another thing on her list. And it was about as red as you could get. And she loved it.

Dan stood by him as Micky got in and out of the car, going to the backseat then to the front again. She was trying out all the gadgets—Dan had given her the keys to it—and Micky was happy with them as well. Lucas looked over at Dan and saw

119

that he was enjoying Micky's antics as well.

"As I'm sure you know, we'll take it." Dan nodded, not taking his eyes off Micky. "I'd like the same car, only in black. Do you have one of those in that color?"

"We have a dark blue one. It hasn't been unloaded — She certainly is a delight, is she not? I don't think I've ever seen a person happier with a purchase than she is. Lady Manning should go about town, introduce herself around. Some are saying that you married a prude." Dan looked at him. "Oh my God, I cannot believe that I said that to you. Please forgive me, sir. It wasn't my intention of saying anything like that to you."

"It's all right. And you're absolutely right. We both need to get out more and see the people. Micky has gone through a great deal since we were married. One of her sisters recently passed away, and her mother and other sister they're going to prison." Dan said he was sorry for her loss. "Thank you. I'll tell her for you. And if you'll figure out what we owe you, we'll be out of your hair."

"I've enjoyed it, sir. I was upset at first, her telling me those things. But then I realized that she was right. That was exactly what I was thinking and what I wanted to do. I think I'll sell more cars, believe it or not, if I just let people to come to me after checking on them." Lucas told him that was a great strategy. "Yes, I do believe you might be right on that. I have been too pushy for some time, I think. It could be the reason my sales have been down. I'm going to take her advice and run with it."

Lucas contacted Tristan who said that he was downtown, working on getting supplies for his new classroom. He said he'd be happy to drive his truck to his house so long as he brought him back. After paying for the cars via the bank, Micky drove off the lot minutes before he did. It was fun watching her be so happy with something.

After both of them pulling into the garage, they made their way to the house. Tristan showed up about ten minutes later. He was as happy as Micky had been about her car.

"You have to come see it, Tristan. It's beautiful, and it's so nice. Red too. I so wanted a red car." She let him start it up to play as she had done. "You will need one soon as well. Driving back and forth to the high school, it'll be easier than having to haul everything in your truck. But you have to use Dan as the salesperson you work with. He's turning over a new leaf, and I want him to succeed."

"Is he giving you part of his commission for helping him out?" They all three laughed and Tristan joined them for lunch. Lucas had hoped that he could persuade Micky into a little more fun, but having his brother there, and happy, was well worth having to put it off. "I'm buying supplies that they told me that I would need. Also, they gave me a list of supplies that the kids would need. Not just for my class, but for all of them. What do you think they'd say if I donated all the things on each of the lists, so that families can be less stressed about buying supplies?"

"I think they'd be very happy with such a great influx of supplies. But you have to be careful, I think. Once you start buying things for them, the board might expect you to buy other items that they need." Tristan asked Micky why she thought that. "Because everyone is greedy. Well, not everyone, but enough to take advantage of your good nature. And your kindness. That's why I never told anyone how much money I have, or about the property. I had people come up to me after Great Grandda died and say that he'd promised this or that. I knew better, so I just got me a job and let people think what they wanted. They were anyway, so this helped me too."

"I can see that happening. All right, my dear. I will hold off buying anything unless I'm sure that it is needed, and that it will be used for the children and not the people who run things for them." Tristan grinned at him. "You, my dear brother, have a very intelligent wife. I can only hope that mine is just like her."

"She'll come along and nab you when you least expect it." Micky laughed as Lucas did because of the look on Tristan's face. "I hope she's a ball buster too. That way she can keep you on your toes all the time. I know that you need that."

Lucas took his brother back to the parking lot of the school where he'd left his own truck. He didn't get out right away, so he waited on him. Tristan had always been a quiet thinker, and when he spoke, like they did with Cooper, people listened.

"I've had my house redone. Walls painted. Even putting some of the things that I've had forever in it as well. It's large enough for me to need a staff, so I hired some." Lucas wasn't sure where this was going but said that was a good idea. "Do you think she'll be a ball buster, Lucas? I'm not the kind of man that those sort of women like. I'm too...I guess you'd call it timid. I avoid conflict as much as I possibly can. I don't need a woman that is going to put me in my place."

"I think I thought the same thing. And Micky is timid as well. But when she needs to be, she can be just as scary as we are as our dragons. And I love that about her." Tristan nodded, and they both watched as teachers went in and out of the building in anticipation of the new school year. "She'll fit you, Tristan. Whoever or whatever she is, you will blend together and be as solid in your life as I feel mine is."

Tristan got out of the car then but stood at the open window. When Tristan smiled at him, he had a feeling that he'd figured out something. And he was as positive as he was of his love for Micky that it was going to backfire on him.

When he walked away, Lucas sat there for a few moments and turned home when he thought of what he was going to do to Micky. He was hard too, just thinking about her. Lucas hoped there weren't any more visits to their home today. He had a plan.

went into their bedroom. Lucas had his back to her, pouring something in tall glasses. From where she was standing, she thought it was champagne. It hadn't been up here before, so she figured that he'd had the staff do it. Clearing her throat, she watched him turn to her slowly, holding a glass in his right hand.

The glass breaking scared her a little. But when Lucas just stood there, staring at her, Micky started to fidget. He still hadn't moved, nor had he said anything about breaking one of the glasses. She was going to get dressed and leave. This was just—

"You look like every wet dream I've ever had. Not only are you sexy, but you're lovely too." He took several steps toward her, halving the distance between them. "I don't know where to start on worshipping your body. Where to touch you first. I've thought of you all day and how I was going to take you. But you did so much better than I could have. You've become perfect. Just for me."

"That was beautiful." He leaned down to kiss her and she licked his lips with her tongue. "You taste so delicious. Like cream and honey. As if you've just nibbled on a scone."

"I did before coming here." He kissed her throat, setting the area on fire. "You taste wanton. Like all the sexiness of the world has settled over you. And you're all mine."

No more words were spoken then. He gently took off her nightie, pulling the small strings that held the panties. As soon as she was naked from the waist down, she felt her pussy run hot, her cream sliding down her legs.

With a smile, Lucas dropped down to his knees and kissed her hips, her navel, as well as her thighs. But he didn't touch her the way that she wanted, needed, and it was on the tip of her tongue to tell him to hurry. Then he spread her nether lips and blew a hot flame of breath over her.

Micky screamed then. The climax from what he had done to her made her weak with it. Holding onto his head as he leaned in for more, she cried out again when he licked her nubbin, then took it into his mouth and suckled at her like she was a feast.

Over and over she came, each time sure it was draining her just a little more. And when her knees could no longer hold her upright, she crumbled to the floor in an exhausted pile of mush.

"No more."

He was naked, and his hard body had a slight dew of sweat all over him. When he held his cock in his hand, fisting it back and forth, her body was invigorated, ready for him to take her over again. Reaching for him, she cried out when he bit her hard on the shoulder.

The pain was only for a moment, then it was gone. Wrapping her legs around his waist when he helped her, Micky felt the heat of his cock, the way that it touched off nerve endings all over her body. Even her hair felt like it was alive. And when he entered her, Micky blacked out for a second or two.

"I need you." She nodded at him, his voice sounding dark and promising. And when he took her hard, bringing her to peak four times, she felt the moment that he came. Lucas threw back his head, his body bent so much that she was sure that he'd hurt himself. Then he took her harder, pounding her hard enough that she moved across the floor.

When he came this time, it was like he'd filled her with lava; his climax, even harder than the one before it, took her breath away. And when he shouted out again, declaring his love for her for all eternity, Micky came with him, holding onto him for fear that she'd fly away.

Waking up in the bed, Lucas was curled around her. He was sleeping so peacefully that she watched him. To her he was

128

the most handsome man alive. And he would be the only one that would ever hold her heart.

She'd thought about Richard a lot lately, mostly comparing him to Lucas, recognizing things that had irritated her even then about the man she had been about to marry. The way he ate his food with his mouth open, blaming it on the sinus trouble that he wouldn't have treated. He would also take the most of whatever they were sharing. Popcorn at the movies and at home. The times that he had taken all the covers and blamed her for not being aggressive enough to take them back from him. Not really big things, and things that she could have lived with, but now that she knew what true love was, how it felt to be cherished by someone, to have her every whim taken care of, she knew that she would have been miserable for a very long time with Richard.

Carson had told her yesterday that she thought that Mariam the Second had killed him. She was looking into it, putting all the information together to give to the district attorney that was prosecuting her sister. And later that night, Winnie told her that not only had Mariam killed him, but she had killed two other people. Winnie had read her mind and found the evidence on what had to be done to bring her to justice for the murders.

Touching Lucas, his mouth and his brow, Micky wondered if he'd been told that they'd killed. He more than likely did know and was waiting for a time when she wasn't as upset as she'd been over the last few days. It had been hard, profoundly so, to deal with all her family again. But she had to admit, it was much easier with him beside her.

Looking at him again, she saw that he'd awoken. When he smiled at her, Micky felt like the sun was shining just for her. And the flowers in the gardens were beautiful because she was so very happy.

"You're thinking very hard. What's wrong?" She told him what was on her mind. "I'm sorry that you lost him. But I'm glad that you were made aware that your sister was involved in his death. Your family has been nothing but pains in the ass for a very long time. And I, for one, am very glad that they're getting their comeuppance."

"I love you, Lucas. I'm so happy that you came barging into my life." He laughed when she did, then kissed her on the nose. When he sat on the side of the bed, he was dressed in jeans and a T-shirt. "Are you leaving me?"

"No. God no. I found out from Xavier that there are two children in need of a home. They're six months and five years old. Their parents were killed when they OD'ed a few days ago. The neighbor said that she'd not seen them in a while and called the police." Getting up, she was dressed as well. "I thought if you were serious about wanting children now, that we'd go and see them. No obligation, but just a visit to see how they're faring."

"You know as well as I do that we're bringing them home with us. What do we have to do to make the transition from there to here?" He stood up and grinned at her. "Well, Dad, what do we do?"

"I've been meaning to help you out with something for days now. And Rose, the faerie that belongs to Cooper, reminded me that you need a faerie. Grace couldn't decide on which one she wanted, so she had a few of them come to you. While that's all right for now, I'd only take one." She asked him why he was bringing that up now. "Because they're magical too. I mean, more so than any other faerie, because they belong to a dragon family."

"And who do you have picked out for me? You know, I've been meaning to ask you about the one that follows you all the time. I'm assuming that he belongs to you?" He said that he did. And his name was Tucker. "I see. Where are they now?"

He opened the window, and three of the most beautiful creatures flittered in front of her face. She knew Rose, so she asked her what she needed to do. This was her first time with a small creature.

"One will be with you at all times when you are out of the house or just out of the bedroom. We only enter that room when you call out to us. Then you'll be safe." She nodded and looked at the other two. "This is Nate, and the female is Hail. Like the hard rain. She was born then and has adopted the name."

"I see. And these two, what do I have to do to pick one? And just so you know, I'm not keen on picking someone to be my slave." Rose assured her that it was an honor to be chosen by the dragon family. "All right. Can they both hang around with me? So I can figure out which one suits me more?"

"Nay, my lady. If you take the two of them, they will belong to you and no other. Even should you not pick one of them, they will never be able to go with another person again." Rose bowed. "If you wish, they both will stay with you. And you will find that they can be most helpful when you need it. I'm to understand that you're going to see to some young children? These two can ready a room for you with all that you need. The queen will also pick a faerie for each of the children which will keep them safe as well."

She liked the idea of someone watching over the kids. Micky wasn't positive that they'd come home with them, but they'd be ready for any that came to them.

"All right then. I'd like for you to ready a room for the children. They're not very old. Lucas told me that they were five years and just six months. I forgot to ask him what their sexes were, so can we make it sort of neutral for now?" They both nodded and said that it would be their pleasure to do so. "I think I'd like to have them close to us. I don't know anything about how they're going to be, but I'd as soon have them close to us to comfort them. They've more than likely gone through a lot."

"You have nothing to worry about here, my lady. We'll be ready for them no matter what they're going to need." She thanked them both and Rose left them. Micky turned to them both, thanking them again for taking on this task. "We have done this before, so we are well versed in what a child will need when they're so young."

"I forgot to ask how I pay you." Hail told her that flowers would be the best. And sugar cubes when she was most pleased with them. "I can do that for you. Thank you again for your help. We'll be back as soon as we can. We hope with the children."

"Us too, my lady. We'll be ready for your return. And if you'd wait but a moment or two, we'll have a bag for you to take with you to see them. Hail will see to the car seats for them."

Again, they made things easier for her. She might like this having someone around all the time. It had already come in handy in the last few minutes.

~*~

Mariam sat in her cell. Bethany was gone? She couldn't believe it. As her mother, someone should have told her that her darling baby had been sick. Mariam laid down on the bed, her heart broken for her child, when she heard Me-Me calling her name. Turning to look at her without getting up, she asked her what she wanted.

"You don't believe her, do you? I mean, don't you think that Bethany would have told us that she was ill? And she'd only been in this place for a couple of weeks. How could they have found it here, and her be dead in that short time?" Mariam

132

said she didn't know but did believe that she was gone. "You're going to take the word of that bitch? Mother, she's just trying her best to hurt us."

"Yes, I believe her. And for as much as you hate her, as do I, I wouldn't believe her to be that cruel to us, telling us that my baby is gone. She is a lot of things, I will say that, but not bad enough to say that someone was gone if they weren't." Mariam wiped at the tears. She had done this, her and the other two. They had made it so that neither of them could be beside Bethany when she took her last breath. "She didn't have to come and tell us either. Micky did that, for us."

"Are you trying to suck up to her? It won't work, Mother. Micky has no heart in her. She'd just as soon have us rolling in the mud rather than help us. Believe me, I've tried to get her to do it."

Mariam said nothing as she lay there. Me-Me was still talking, but she was no longer listening to her.

Her child was gone. Bethany had never been like her and Me-Me. She'd gone along with things, even if she didn't care for them. But she wasn't one to get vengeance on anyone, and had been, when she was little, such a happy baby.

Mariam was thinking about all the things that they'd done as a family, always keeping their plans from Micky. So many times, they'd gone on shopping sprees, out to lunch, and stayed at expensive hotels just because they knew that Micky wasn't joining them. Mariam for a moment wished that she could do this all over.

"Mariam Mantle?" She stood up when the man's voice echoed through her cell. He had on a suit and tie, so that meant he wasn't working here. "My name is Winston Sheppard. I'm your court appointed lawyer."

"Thank you." She was let out of her cell, and they went to a room that was used for this kind of conversation, she supposed. "I'd like to...before I change my mind, I'd like to confess to everything they have on me and more."

"Confess? I thought that you were pleading not guilty on all charges. And I have to admit, ma'am, there are a great many charges against you. Murder for one, theft for another. And a slew of others that are just as serious." Mariam thought of her life, how she'd come to be where she was. While she didn't hate herself, she wasn't very proud of herself either.

"My daughter died, so we were told. Is that true?" He handed her the newspaper that was folded to the obituary page. There it was, confirmation that her little girl had died of cancer. "I could have been with her when she died. But I was a fool and was here instead of taking care of her. Can you tell me, please, where she spent her final days?"

"It is my understanding that she was staying at the home of Lord Lucas and Lady Micky Manning's home. She did have the best of care while there. They had set up a room for her, so she could have peace as well as all the medications that she'd need." She asked him how he knew this. "My wife, she helps people that need special equipment in their home for cases like this one."

Micky had been with her. Even after all that they'd done to her, she had opened her home to her sister, and even made sure that she had everything that she needed. With more resolve than she had before, Mariam straightened her back and looked at the man in front of her. She'd do this, right now because it was the right thing to do.

"I do wish to confess to everything. If you would, I'd like for you to make a list for me, I'll give you the names of the people that I worked with, how I had come to meet them, and how we had been criminals." He asked if he could record her.

"Yes, that'll be fine. I might not put them in order, but you can fix that too. Correct?"

"Yes. But Ms. Mantle, are you sure that you wish to do this? As I said, there are a great many things on this list already. You would be looking at a very long life in prison, if you ever got out." She nodded; it was time for her to pay for the crimes she'd committed. "All right then. I'll do what you want."

Mr. Sheppard let her speak, only asking her questions to clarify some of the details. She was brought her dinner as well as extra water. When she had filled two of the tiny little tapes that he had, she felt drained, yet better for having gotten it off her chest.

"Ms. Mantle, I'm going to have my secretary type this up for you, and I'll bring it back tomorrow for you to read over and sign." She said that she had nowhere to go. "All right. I can bring you in a few things, nothing illegal however. Would you like some magazines or some books to read? I would be happy to bring them when I come back."

"If you could, I'd like to have one of those little cards that are printed up for funerals. And a picture of her gravesite if you can manage that. I want to be able know that she's really gone from me. I know you were kind enough to bring the paper, but I'd like those things as well." He told her that her daughter, Lady Micky, had wanted her to have the paper as well as a few other things. He pulled out the other things that Micky had sent her.

There were pictures of Bethany out in the yard. She was sitting in a wheelchair, her hair pulled back. The picture showed how weak she had been, how frail she had looked. Even her smile seemed to be sad.

"I've missed so much being what I was. My daughter dying, it's what brought me around to confessing to you." She looked through the pictures, about two dozen of them, that had been in an envelope. There were even photos of Bethany when she'd been a baby, ones of her birthday party when she'd turned five, with Me-Me hogging the frame. There were a few of Christmas, some of when they were at the beach. And in all of them, there wasn't a sign of Micky. Mariam wasn't even sure that she'd been at any of these events. They'd sneak off and leave her at home when they went out. "I've been so horrible to her. Yet she saw to it that I knew that Bethany had died and gave me these things to remember her by. I can't tell you how stupid I was. And that I was such a fool."

"She asked me to tell you something, but only if you asked. Lady Micky said that she can forgive you for what you did to her. And she would make sure, when your time comes, that you're next to Bethany. But she will never come to visit either of you."

Nodding, she sat there and cried hard. She was handed a box of tissues and held them like a lifeline. It was what she deserved. Even with everything she'd done to Micky—and there had been a great many of them—she was willing to make sure that she'd be next to Bethany.

On her way back to her cell, she sobbed. Her life was ending. She might not die right away—Mariam thought that she'd more than likely live a very long time, just so she could get the full treatment of being in prison. When the door slid closed, the sound of it much like a gun going off, Mariam laid down on her bed with the pictures and newspaper clutched to her heart. What a fool she'd been.

Mariam heard another man come back and tell Me-Me that he was her attorney. Of course, she had to bitch about how he'd taken so long, that she wanted him to get her nicer clothing as well as better food. As far as Mariam was concerned, she was eating better in here than she ever had when she'd been out in the real world. Me-Me returned a short time later and was locked in her cell again.

"Mom, I think I have a way for us to get out of here. Are you game?" Mariam rolled to her back and looked at her daughter. "I know a few people that can sneak us out of here, no trouble. You be ready when—"

"No. I'm not leaving here with you. I confessed to all my crimes, and I'm going to pay for it with my life." Me-Me asked her if she was stupid. "No. I was before today, very much so. But now I'm working on owning up to what I've done. Bethany is really gone, Me-Me. Micky opened her house for her to come live with her in her final days. She even sent me pictures of her, and some from—"

"You confessed? Are you stupid? If you confess, Mother, they're going to put you away forever. Fuck that shit. I'm going down swinging." Mariam told her good luck with that, but she wasn't going to go with her. "You're just saying that now because your heart hurts. In a couple of days, you'll see. I'll get us both out of here. And we'll hit Micky up for some cash. Enough to get us out of the country."

Me-Me continued to make plans, shouting some of them in her direction. Mariam didn't listen. She wasn't going to recant her confession, nor was she going to get out of here with Me-Me. She might be too late on a lot of things, but she wasn't going to be looking over her shoulder for the rest of her life either.

Chapter 10

The hospital where the children were was warm. There were pictures on the wall that were bright and happy. Lucas wasn't paying much attention to the things—he was more concerned about seeing the kids. Micky was holding his hand so tightly that he was sure that she was going through the same anxiety he was.

Lucas smiled at the woman at the big desk in the center of the room. "We're the Mannings. I think my brother made arrangements for us to come and see the orphans that were just brought in." The nurse, Wanda her badge said, smiled at them with a big toothy grin. "They're all right, aren't they?"

"Right as rain. We were just trying to get the little girl to eat something. She's still having a difficult time of it. The baby, another little girl, is too young to remember much about her home life and ate well." Wanda led them to the back end of the hallway. "They've both had baths—you'd not believe the number of bruises and hurts we had to take care of. They had nothing with them when they arrived here for a checkup. Amber, the oldest, she's got a ragged teddy bear that smells

139

like she might have picked it up at the dump. But she won't let go of it."

"How much do they know about their parents?" Micky watched the children that were playing in a large area as she asked questions. Lucas could tell right away which one Amber was. She was sitting in the corner as far away from the other children as she could get. He asked to go into the room.

"Don't be surprised if she screams at you to go away. She's not been sexually abused, thank the good Lord, but she's been abused all the same." He nodded and was let in the room with her. Micky was right behind him. He sat down on the floor in front of Amber and she looked at him, then away.

"My name is Lucas Manning. My wife is Micky. We've come to talk to you." Amber asked where Mary Anne was. "Your sister? She's being cared for in another part of the hospital."

"I have to watch her." Lucas said that he knew that she was doing a good job too. "Those people that came to get us, they took my sister away and wouldn't let me see her. I have to watch over her."

"All right. How about I have them bring Mary Anne here so that you can be with her? Would you like that?" She eyed him carefully and he felt his dragon curl around him. He wanted to protect her too. "If you'd talk to my wife for a few moments, I'll see what I can do."

It took him the better part of an hour to get the baby brought to them. There was red tape out the ass, and he hated every second of it. But every time he looked, Amber and Micky seemed to be getting along well. When he was taken to the nursery and the baby put into a cart-like bassinet, he took her to the little room that Amber had been brought to.

As soon as Amber was able to hold the baby, she seemed to light up. The baby too. They had missed each other, and he was glad that he could give them this little bit of comfort. While Amber talked softly to her sister, he reached out to Micky and asked her what she thought.

They're both going to need someone to talk to. Maybe not the infant, but for sure, Amber. She's the one that found her parents. Amber told me that she was glad they were gone, that they'd hurt her all the time. He had already figured that out when he'd read over the report while waiting on the okay to get Mary Anne. *Do you think we can take them home today? I so want to get them out of here. This is no place for a child that is hurting as she seems to be.*

I agree, honey. I think I can pull a few strings to see if we can do that. According to the doctor that treated them, they're both in good health, but Amber is underweight for her age.

Micky said that they'd get her fattened up. Lucas laughed. *I guess that is the wrong thing to say to a dragon.*

It's fine — funny though.

He stood up and told them all that he'd be back. As soon as he could find their doctor, he was going to take his children home with him. At least he hoped so. If not, he'd sic one of the women of his family on him.

He made his way to the front desk. "I'm looking for Doctor Fleming."

"She's just come on duty, Lord Manning." He nodded. Lucas wondered when the village as a whole would start to call them mister, or even by their first names. Sitting in one of the soft chairs, he waited for the doctor. "I let her know that you are here and told her that you're here for the children. To have them go to such a good home, I'm so happy for them."

"Thank you very much. I only hope that everyone sees this as a good move for them." He really wasn't worried about them having a background check. They both had their own money, jobs that they were proud of, as well as a family dynamic that was strong and tight.

He felt so embarrassed when he met with the doctor. He'd been dozing in the chair, it had been that comfortable. After telling her what they wanted to do, Lucas followed her to her office.

"I'm going to be honest with you, Lord Manning, I'd love nothing more than to turn them over to you. But there is a holdup on this. It's your wife's family, and the trouble that they have been in lately." He assured her that they'd never be around the children, as they were set for prison. "Be that as it may, we still have to consider that. I've sent through the application already. Lady Carson called here and told me that you'd be in to take them. She's somewhat scary, isn't she?"

"Yes. But loveable. They have their own children from someone that passed away. The mother had cancer throughout her body and had called Cooper when she needed someone to take over raising her sons." She said that she remembered that. "If you don't mind me asking, what will it take to see to it that they come home with us?"

"I've already filled out the paperwork for the adoption and asked that you and your wife be foster parents for the two of them. It's the best I can do under the circumstances."

He would take whatever he could get at this point. Lucas knew that they'd have to have a good showing to make this work. He only hoped that Micky's mother and sister made it to prison, and for a very long time.

Lucas looked up when Doctor Fleming's phone rang at her desk at the same time his own cell phone went off. Standing up and moving to the other side of the room, he answered his cell. It was Winnie, and she was laughing when he answered. Saying her name, he wasn't surprised when she told him to fuck off and to wait. Such a charmer his sister-in-law was.

"Okay. I've pulled some strings, made a few people see reason. I'm pretty good at being nice. But don't think that it's going to happen again." He told her he wouldn't and what was she talking about. "Your doc is getting a call from some important people. They just love you Mannings and what you've done for the community. That the children couldn't be with better people if she were to put out a list of the perfect parents."

"I don't know what to say. You've done something extremely nice for Micky and me. I can't—I have no idea how I can ever repay you for this." She told him not to stress over it, that she'd enjoyed it. "Thank you again, Winnie. If you ever need anything, and I do mean anything, you'll have it."

"I have all I ever needed in the form of your brother. He makes me happy and satisfied with life." Winnie cleared her throat before continuing. "Hudson and I, we're thinking of doing what you guys are doing. Taking children not just to our home, but our hearts too. Okay, enough mushy stuff. I'll talk to you later."

When she closed the connection to their call, Lucas stood where he was and thought about Winnie and what she'd done for them. He swore he'd find a way to repay her for this, even if he had to kill someone for her. Why she'd need him to do something that she was better at than anyone else, he had no idea, but he'd do it. Laughing a little, he noticed that Doctor Fleming was finished with her call as well.

"I've just had a call from the mayor. He had company at his house and heard that you and Lady Manning were wanting to take the children home with you. His company was the governor. He, too, gave the two of you glowing recommendations. And they told me to put the paperwork through to them and they'd sign off on the adoption. You have some pretty powerful friends, Lord Manning." He told her that he did but hadn't expected that. "No, he said that you wouldn't. Told me that if they had any children that were misplaced in their homelife, to call your family to see if you could take them as well. I don't think you'll have any issues going forward, and you can take them home with you."

"Thank you so much." She told him that Amber would have to see someone that could help her. "Yes, my wife and I were discussing that very thing. Thank you, Doctor Fleming. And if you need something that we can get for your hospital, then you've only to call."

"Thank you. I will hold you to that. We're a small hospital here and getting the things that we need to keep people healthy and happy—we could use some equipment." He told her to give him a list and his family would work on it. "Thank you so much. You have no idea how much we need any one of the things I'll give you on this list. Thank your family for me as well."

Lucas was nearly giddy when he made his way back to the pediatric area. As he walked along the halls, he could see what the doctor was talking about. Some of the walls had water damage. The floors had missing or broken tiles. Even the desk that he was at had a computer that looked like it was new in the eighties. As soon as they got home and settled, he was going to call a family meeting and see what they could do about this.

We get to take them home with us. And the adoption is in the bag as well. Winnie helped with it, and if you don't mind, I don't want to ask her about it.

Micky told Amber where they were going. Micky was holding Mary Anne, but Amber was keeping a watchful eye on her.

Lucas stooped down in front of Amber. "There are all kinds

of people you get to meet. I have five brothers and three sisters-in-law. They are all excited to meet you two."

"I don't want to go." He had anticipated this. The child was terrified out of her mind and would balk at being taken away from the hospital. Especially since it more than likely had been the only safe place they'd ever been. "You aren't going to make me either."

Before he could speak, Micky did. "All right. You don't have to go. But since Mary Anne is an infant and not able to make her own decisions, I'm making them for her. She can't stay here. And when they think that you're ready to be released, you'll go to a family that could be as bad as the one you lived with. You should also be aware that you might be separated from each other forever. Your adoption might take you far away, and you'd not be able to see her every day. Like you can at our house."

Amber fought tears, but she couldn't hold them back any longer. He was handed Mary Anne and Micky reached for Amber. It was a struggle at first, both of them fighting to get what they wanted. But in the end, Amber let Micky hold her while she sobbed. It broke his heart to hear her crying like that, and it made his dragon roar inside of him with the need to protect her.

In the end, they were able to take both of the little girls home. The car seat for Amber was like a booster type of seat, while the one for Mary Anne was facing backward, and she fit perfectly in it. They were given a list of things that the baby would need, as well as the type of formula that they had been feeding her. Amber was quiet all the way to the car. Lucas had to stand outside his car for a few moments. He was a father.

"You all right?" Nodding at Micky, he noticed that she hadn't gotten into the car either. "I'm not. I'm a mom, and I

145

haven't the slightest idea how to go about that."

"That's pretty much what I was thinking. I hope we don't mess them up." Micky said she thought they'd be fine at this. "Really? Because all I can think about right now is I'm a dad. You're a mom."

"We'll be fine. I'm sure of it. And we have Hail and Tucker to keep us straight on all this, right?" Lucas was basing his ability to raise two children on faeries that were smaller than his hand. "Come on, Dad, let's get the kids home. I, for one, am excited for this new venture."

He was too, but that didn't make him any less terrified. While they were driving home, he tried to engage Amber in conversation, but she just answered him in single words. He knew it would get better, but right now he felt as if he had failed her in some way. Lucas knew that he'd not, but it was the unknown that was making him feel this way.

~*~

Me-Me couldn't get her mom to answer her. She'd been lying on her bed since she'd spoken to her attorney yesterday. Me-Me had no idea what had happened in there, but she was going to make someone pay for her mother acting this way. Surely, she hadn't confessed to everything like she said she had. Mom would be in prison for sure if they only knew a part of what she'd done and done with Me-Me as well.

When their lunch was brought in, her mom got up and stared at it for several seconds before she laid back down. Even with Me-Me shouting at her to answer her, she didn't even look her way. This was bad. Whatever was going on, it was making her nervous. Me-Me began to wonder what kind of confessions her mother had made. Did she tell on her? Were the attorneys for the other side calculating how much time she was going to spend in prison with her mom? Me-Me wouldn't let herself

146

believe that her mother had sold her up the river.

Giving up on getting her mom to talk to her, she watched her as her mind was working on how to get out. This place followed rules that she'd never heard of. Me-Me was sure that they were making some of them up. Like not being allowed to go outside for a little while. They had to change their own sheets and return them to the guard that stood there. And the shower.

She'd been mortified when she was stripped of her clothing and shoved into a shower stall. There wasn't a curtain that she could close for privacy; the female guard that had brought her there stood right outside the stall and watched her every move. Me-Me wondered if they thought that she could travel very far with chains on her ankles. And no amount of begging could get her anything to wear that several hundred people had not worn before her.

After being given a towel that was thinner than the toilet paper, she was handed a clean but still orange one piece to put on. She'd given up on asking for something better. Not that she thought she was superior than anyone else — she knew she was, really — but it was terrible for her complexion. Of course, Me-Me hadn't been visited by anyone since her sister had come by to tell them about Bethany.

She missed her sister. Bethany hadn't been as adventurous as she'd been. Me-Me would have to bully or even beat her into submission to go along with whatever Me-Me found to be daring. That was what life was about, trying it all and going to your grave as an old yet satisfied person.

But life hadn't been satisfying for her. Me-Me had two children, and didn't want them around, except when she wanted to show off. Only the two children, but she had made up for her lack of more children when it came to husbands. Or in her case, ex-husbands. She had seven so far. Me-Me wondered if, when she got out of here, there would be a sucker out there that could give her what she wanted. And Me-Me wanted it all.

At about one, they came and picked up the trays and commented on her mom's. She heard her tell the guard that she wasn't hungry, and the guard left them. But another guard came back as soon as the trays were gone to tell Me-Me that she had a visitor. Her attorney.

Yesterday she'd tried to talk him into having sex with her for payment in getting her out of here. He'd declined so loudly that the guards had come in to see what was the matter. Mr. Daily didn't tell them what had happened, but he did warn her to behave herself or he'd quit her. Like she was paying him or something, and he was going to quit a job that he'd been assigned.

Mr. Daily was sitting in the chair that he'd been in the other day, with another man sitting next to him. This man was dressed in an expensive suit, his tie matching his shirt like he'd ordered it that way. Me-Me smiled at them both as she was sat down and chained to the table.

"I hope you have good news today. I really want to get out of here as soon as possible. My sister died recently, and I need to make sure that the arrangements for her have been met." It was a lie. She knew that if Micky was in charge, it would have been done perfectly. But it pissed her off that Micky had done it without consulting her. The second man pulled out a file from his briefcase. "What's the deal with you both being here? Are you really quitting me like you threatened the other day?"

"No, I'm here to advise you on things. Not that I think you'll listen—you haven't so far. But this is Attorney General Marcus Turner. He's here to ask you a few questions." Me-Me told him that was all right. "You do understand that you cannot lie to him concerning this? You have to tell him the truth about everything that he asks you."

"I understand that you're talking too much and not saying what I want you to say. When am I getting out? You have avoided that question for long enough. Mom might have confessed to a lot of shit, but I had nothing to do with any of it." The Turner man cleared his throat and asked if she was ready. "Sure, go for it."

"The first thing I'd like to tell you is that this entire interview is being recorded. Both with sound and video. Do you understand that?" Me-Me nodded. "I need a verbal answer, Ms. Patterson, on this and all questions."

"Yes, I understand. Get on with it already. I want to go home. I have to see my sister." He asked her if this was Micky Manning. "I guess it's her. I know she got married recently, which will never last, but I didn't catch her last name."

He pulled out a single sheet of paper. Me-Me couldn't read it upside down like it was, but she could make out that it was a numbered list. It was a long one too. Whatever it said, she knew it wasn't going to go good for her.

"Your mother, Mariam Mantle, has signed a written confession about all the crimes that she has committed. At her trial, the list she gave us will be read to the judge by me, and he'll decide what happens to her as for sentencing. I believe that she will be put away for a very long time." Me-Me was all right with that, so long as it didn't affect her getting out of there. "She named you as an accomplice to a great many of these crimes. She even gave us enough details that we were—"

"Just hold on a fucking minute. What do you mean, she told you that I helped her kill people? I didn't. Whatever she said, it's nothing to do with me." He told her that he'd not mentioned any murders. Me-Me was suddenly seeing the big

149

picture here. "She didn't have my permission to name me in anything that I didn't do with her."

"She didn't need it. She confessed to a great many things, including murder, and she told us that you were involved in nearly all of it." Me-Me looked at her attorney. She thought for sure he should be doing something right now. "We have enough information to go to the places that you buried your victims. They are being exhumed as we speak. So far, on two of the deaths that she told us you were helping her in, we found enough DNA and fingerprints on the murder weapons to know that you were there."

"I don't know what you're talking about. Maybe she put it there to get me into trouble." She laughed, and even to her ears, it sounded manic. "Can you believe this shit? A mother pinning things on her own child? I'm appalled at this. I would like to go back to my cell, so I can ask her about it."

"Your mother was taken to the courthouse to hear her judgment. Since she confessed to it all, there will not be any need for a trial. We've worked to make it so that she is going to prison today, if we can manage it. But we're here about you and what you've done. I'd like you to go over the list that your mother gave us, and tell us your involvement in each one you're named in."

The list, even turned around, was difficult to read. She was angry. Her head was in pain from this. Then she was able to make out the first incident, when she'd been just eighteen. It mentioned how she and her mother rolled an elderly man for enough cash for them to celebrate her getting out of school. The man died later as a result of what they'd done to him.

Me-Me read each one, denying any involvement in any of it. When she was finished, Me-Me was wondering what they'd do now when her attorney stood up. The other man, Turner, did as well, and told her guy that he'd step out for a moment.

Her attorney sat down and didn't say anything for a long while. It made her nervous again, and she lashed out at him to tell him to say something. When he laughed a little, Me-Me wondered if this entire thing was a joke. But then he spoke to her.

"You will be put to death for your crimes. I'm sure that once you are before a jury, they'll see you as you are—a woman who did anything to get whatever she wanted. And not only that, but Ms. Mantle has implicated you in just about everything that she was found guilty of." Me-Me didn't know what to say. She felt as if she was underwater with no way to get up to where the air was. "If I were you, I'd plead guilty to all of it. Even if you don't remember any of the things that are on that list, they're going to blame you for it. But even by pleading guilty, Ms. Patterson, I don't know if it will save you from being executed."

"This isn't right. You know that, don't you? I shouldn't be in here. I don't want to be in here. Don't you see? My sister is gone, and now this." He said that this was there long before her sister had died. "Micky did this, didn't she? She made Mother confess to all kinds of shit so that we'd be out of her life. I'm going to make her pay as soon as I get out of here."

"You're not getting out. Going to trial or not is going to be the difference in how you get to spend the rest of your life—either living in prison or ending it very soon. I would suggest you plead guilty to make it look like you're somewhat be repentant for what you've done." She told him she wasn't going to do that. "Then may God have mercy on your soul. You are signing your own death warrant."

Me-Me didn't see when the Turner guy came back in the room with them. All she could think about was that her mother had sold her up the river without a paddle. And if she did

151

confess, like they wanted her to do, she'd never be able to show her face in the country club again. Me-Me decided that she was going to be on her best behavior while she was in prison so that she could get out early. That way, she could take care of Micky when she got out. Me-Me looked at her attorney.

"Yes, I'll confess. I'll do it so that I can get out someday. And I will."

Neither of them said anything but handed her the paper again. Signing her name across the bottom, she was helped up and led back to her cell. Her mother was gone. The cell was like hers had been when she'd first gotten here—the mattress folded over and no sheets on it.

Sitting on her bed, she thought about what she'd just done—signed a part of her life away. When she made her way to the courtroom, whenever that was, she was going to put her best foot forward. That way, they'd lessen the sentence. Me-Me had no idea if that would work or not, but she was going to do it. Even if it killed her.

Chapter 11

Micky showed Amber around the house. Twice she got turned around in the mammoth place, but it seemed to tickle Amber. She'd get lost a million times just to hear her laughter again. They ended their tour on the second floor to show her the room that the faeries had set up for her. Micky was almost jealous that she couldn't sleep in this room.

"I didn't know what you wanted to do about your sister. She can bunk in here with you, or we have a nice nursery set up just next door to you." Amber went around the room, her hands linked tightly behind her. "There are some clothes for you as well. Not that many right now—we weren't sure what sort of things you'd like to wear. There aren't any shoes either, for the same reason."

Micky was glad that she had been briefed on what was in the rooms—what Tucker and Hail had taken care of. The room looked beautiful. It hadn't been done in pinks or too many bright colors. Being five years old, Amber would be making her likes of wallpaper and such on her own. Winnie touched her mind just as she was ready to ask Amber what she wanted.

She hasn't a clue that the room and the things in it are for her. Don't tell her that they are, however. Just keep it light. The kid is terrified that you're going to decide to only take care of her sister, and that she'll be in the system. Apparently, she's heard a lot of horror stories about the system, and she doesn't want to go. Micky asked her what she should do. *I think the rest of us girls should come over, load up in cars, and head to the mall. Amber will see you in action and meet the rest of us too. By the way, her faerie is in the room with the two of you. I'd introduce them before we arrive.*

All right. Thanks Winnie. She told her she might not be thanking her when they all came over. *I'm sure that I can handle you guys. Not that you don't scare me a bit, but you're wonderful women.*

Sitting on the bed, she asked Amber to come sit by her. When she said that she'd rather not, Micky told her that she understood. Then she put out her hand and Amber's faerie landed on her hand. With a bow, the tiny creature went to sit on Amber's leg.

"She won't hurt you. I don't know her name, but you can talk to her. You'd think it was hard to hear her, what with her being so small, but you can. Go ahead, ask her who she is." Amber did as she was told but didn't seem all that comfortable with her. "Dilly will be with you at all times. There are times when you won't see her for some reason, but she'll be watching over you. Mary Anne has one as well. But hers, from what I understand, is older, more practiced at watching over babies."

"What is it?" Micky told her that she was a faerie. "I don't believe in them. How are you doing this? Are you trying to trick me?"

"For heaven's sake, no. We're trying to make your transition from the hospital to here better for you." Amber asked her when she was going to leave. "Do you want to leave here? I have no

154

intentions of putting you back in the system. Lucas and I want to be yours and Mary Anne's parents. If you'll let us."

"Nobody wants us." Micky told her that she did, with all her heart. "Our mom and dad, they never told us they loved us or nothing."

"I already love you, Amber. The moment that I saw you, I fell right in love with you. And your little sister is as beautiful as you."

Dilly flittered around Amber until she put out her hand. When she landed there, both of them stared at the other as if they were looking deeply in each other's souls. Amber didn't move when Dilly moved to her shoulder, but Micky could tell that she was excited about the faerie.

"What can they do to keep me safe? I don't think you're going to hurt me, but what if you did?" Micky started to answer her when the women came into the bedroom with them. Amber stood beside Micky and stared at them. "Who are you?"

"We're related to you now." Carson sat down in the chair by the desk while the rest of them sat on the floor. "We're here to tell you a big secret. And we're trusting you to never tell anyone what we tell you. All right?"

Amber didn't answer—she didn't trust them yet. Micky wasn't even sure that she trusted her yet. When she asked them what it was they were going to tell her, Carson took her to the window.

"Do you see him?" Micky went to the window as well and saw Cooper in the yard as his dragon. He was a beautiful sight, and he was much larger than any of the other five. "That's my husband. Would you like to go and meet him? And, so you know, Amber, none of us will ever harm you."

Amber took Micky's hand in hers. Micky felt like she'd just gotten over a large hurdle. And when they made their way out into the yard, Cooper had laid down on the grass and didn't move. He was scary large, and she wasn't sure this was a good idea.

Amber walked right up to the large dragon and put her hand on his nose. She didn't move away from him when Cooper showed her his hand. Amber wasted no time in getting to know his body. She touched all his scales, and when he sat up, Amber easily went into his hand so that he could lift her up to his chest.

"I've never seen a dragon before. Are there a lot of them?" Amber stepped back when the yard was suddenly filled with dragons. All the brothers were coming to meet the newest addition to the family. "Which one is Lucas?"

Micky took her over to where he was and introduced her to his dragon. "We can't have children of our own. The only person that has so far is Carson, and we think it's because she's the queen of all dragons. Her husband, the larger one, is Cooper." Amber looked up at her. "This is why we were so happy to have been called to come and get you and your sister. We want you to be our family. Forever."

The dragons took their other forms then, talking to Amber and answering her questions as she asked them. She didn't seem the least bit intimidated with them. Nor did she seem to be frightened of them. As they loaded up in the cars to go shopping, Lucas told Amber that he'd keep an eye on her sister, but to have a good time.

The mall wasn't busy. There were a few mall walkers going around and groups of women just window shopping. Looking at the map, she wondered where the best place was to buy clothing for a five-year-old. Seeing a couple with children that looked to be about her age, Micky took Amber's hand and they followed them.

"They might be going to the bathroom." Micky laughed

and told her that she needed to go too. "I don't know why you're doing this, Ms. Micky. I'm fine with the stuff that we got from the home."

"They told me that you only got a few shirts, no shorts, and a pair of flip flops. Did you get more later?" Amber told her that she hadn't. "Well, we need to get you ready for school. And then you'll need winter clothing in a few months. Also, we can pick up a few summer things that will be on sale this time of the year. I don't understand that, but I don't shop all that much."

The family that they were following did go into a store. But after one look at the bright pinks and glittery clothing in there, she asked Amber if this was something that she'd like to try on. Winnie came up behind them and put her hand on Amber's shoulder. When she didn't flinch away as she had the first time, she felt they were making progress.

"I don't know. It seems kind of frilly, don't you think?" Winnie agreed with her. "I'd really like a pair of shoes that lace up if you can afford them."

"We can afford anything that you might like. Within reason. What do you say we have lunch and talk about what you want to wear?" They all thought that was a great idea and found a place where they could sit down. "Amber, order whatever you want. This is your day, and we want to have fun."

She eyed the menu like it was going to jump on her and strangle her. It occurred to Micky that she was only five and might not understand what she was seeing. Showing her that she was going to have a cheeseburger and fries with a chocolate malt, Amber said she'd have that too. After that, they were getting along fine.

The shopping had turned into a giggle fest. Amber was showing them things that she didn't want, nor did she want to be out in them, and they laughed with her. The shop that they were in this time was more suited to her. There were jeans that didn't have sparkles on them. And sweaters and shirts that were plain, and again not full of sparkles.

By the time they were all headed back to their cars, Amber had five bags of clothing, two pairs of tennis shoes, some more flip flops, and boots. She had gotten them for her when she kept eyeing them. All in all, it was a very good day. On the way home, Amber sat in the back and stared out the window. Micky wasn't sure what to think about how quiet she'd become until they were in the driveway to their house.

"I don't know why my parents didn't buy us clothing and stuff. I had to steal money for Mary Anne to have diapers and milk to drink. They'd just go to the back porch and get high." Micky sat on the end of her car to listen to her. "We didn't have food a lot of times. Mary Anne was all right because I made sure to bring my milk and stuff home from school for her. And when we didn't have school, it was hard for us. I don't think you'll do that to us, will you?"

"No, never. You and Mary Anne will have the best we can buy for you. You don't ever have to go hungry again. If you want to get up in the middle of the night because you're hungry, you go right ahead. I'll have the cook make sure that there are snacks and sandwiches in the fridge for you." Amber nodded but didn't look at her. "Do you believe me? Do you know that we'd never harm you in any way, and that we'd like for you to be our daughters?"

"Yes." She picked up one of the bags with a large emblem on the front of it. Inside of it were shirts, blouses, as well as underthings. "I've never had a friend. But Winnie, she told me that I had them with her and the rest of the ladies. And she told me that I got the best when it came to having people love you. She said that all of them had already fallen in love with us."

"That's right. I told you, we want you to stay with us forever. Or until you meet someone that you can love too." Amber made a face and they both laughed. "We'd better get this stuff inside and see what Lucas was up to while we were gone. How much do you want to bet that he played with your sister the entire time?"

Lucas not only had played with Mary Anne, but he'd rocked her to sleep in the room's newest rocker. Micky was so excited about having them here. She knew that there would be bumps and hurt feelings, but they'd be a family, and that's what she wanted more than anything.

~*~

The courthouse was packed. Lucas had thought it might be. Mariam the Second had been in the newspaper lately. Mostly it talked about how she had pleaded guilty to a lot of crimes. This would be closure for a lot of deaths too. He'd heard from Hank, the alpha near them, that she'd confessed to at least ten murders. And since she'd confessed to all of them, the trial wasn't necessary. Sentencing would be given to her today.

When they were told to rise, he did too. His entire family was there, supporting Micky in this. She had cried a great deal last night, and today when they'd been ready to go. Amber had hugged her so tightly that it made her cry again—this time with happy tears, she'd told them.

Mariam was brought out of the side door. She was still dressed in her coveralls, and her wrists and ankles were cinched together so that it would be impossible for her to escape. Micky was going to testify against her sister if needed, but he didn't foresee that happening. Lucas knew that was going to cause some trouble.

The attorney that was representing Mariam was sitting two chairs away from his client. He'd heard that she hit him once and had threatened him a few times as well. After she pleaded guilty, however, they said that she'd been a model inmate, not causing any trouble whatsoever. He had an idea why she was doing it, but he kept that to himself. The woman was delusional if she thought she was ever getting out of jail again.

"Ms. Patterson, it is my understanding that you have confessed to your crimes and have been helpful in getting all the information needed to expedite this trial. Is that correct?" Mariam said, "Yes sir," like she was trying to seem meek. "And it is also here that your mother, who is now in the state prison on other charges, has confessed as well. There are several on here that she has implicated you in, as well as several that you did on your own. Is that also true?"

"Yes, sir. It's all true. I was wondering if you could tell me what my bail would be. My sister is here, and I'm sure that if you talk to her, she'll tell you that she'll pay it. My other sister died recently, and I didn't get to go to her funeral or see where she's buried. I have only what Micky says about it." The judge just looked at Mariam. "Micky is right here. She inherited a great deal of money from our great grandda, and she didn't share it with any of us. I think she's spent it all. She'll be good for the money."

"Ms. Patterson, you're not going to have a bail set. You have confessed to several murders, robbery, as well as making and selling methamphetamines. There are also a few areas where you confessed to counterfeiting money." Mariam said that she had, so she should get special treatment for telling them all that. "You are going to jail. Today. And I'm not here to give you any kind of special treatment, nor will you ever get out of prison after what you've done. No bail or bond will ever be set for you."

"But I can get out soon for good behavior, right? I mean,

I'm watching what I say. I've not hit anyone while in there." He mentioned her attorney. "Yes, well, that was before I confessed to things. I've been a good person since I did that other. I'd like for you to tell me how long it will be before I can get out."

"Sit down, Ms. Patterson, and let's get things going." The judge looked at Lucas, and Judge Moody asked for Micky to rise. She was so nervous then that he was sure that she was going to break his hand the way that she was holding it. "Mrs. Manning, it says in my report that you and your family are estranged. Is that correct?"

"Yes, Your Honor. I haven't had anything to do with them since I was a teenager. My mother and two sisters went their own way until they wanted something from me. I never gave in to them except with Beth. She and I talked, and I helped her where I could. My sister is the one that Mariam the Second is referring to. Beth died recently." He said that he was sorry for her loss. "Thank you. It was too late by the time they found her cancer. But we, my family and I, made sure that she was comfortable in her final days."

"She has to help me out. She did Bethany. And that's her name, Micky. How many times do I have to tell you that she's to go by Bethany?" Mariam was told to sit down and be quiet twice before she did. "I just don't understand how she can do things for Bethany and not me."

"Perhaps she came to me asking for forgiveness, and all you've ever done is take and take. You even killed the man that I loved because you were pissed off that I got Great Grandda's estate." Mariam asked her how much of it she had left. "All of it. And I've worked very hard in making more money with it too. My husband and his family and I are adding a new wing to the hospital with the money. All of it. I don't need it. It'll be called the Cain Mantle Wing. Great Grandda would have loved

161

that."

"You'd spend your money on that instead of helping me out? What kind of idiot are you anyway?"

Mariam was told to sit down again, and this time she complied without speaking. The judge just looked around the room at the people there before he spoke again.

"Mariam Mantle Patterson, I've given this a great deal of thought. You've made my decision much easier by your display here today. No one owes you a thing. And the sooner that you get that through your head, the better off you'll be." Mariam said that she was trying. "Yes, well, it's too little too late, I'm afraid. I sentence you to fifty years in prison for each of the murders that you have committed. And you will serve an additional twenty years for making meth with the intent of distributing it. You will also serve an additional thirty-year sentence for counterfeiting. The total number of years you will serve for your crimes consecutively will be three hundred and forty-three years. You have no option for parole at any time. By confessing your crimes, you have saved yourself from being executed. That is all."

"Wait, wait, wait. I don't understand what you are talking about. There isn't anyone alive that can spend three hundred years in prison. You've made a mistake." The judge stood up and so did Mariam. "You have to make it so I can only spend a few years behind bars. I have a lot of things to do yet. And I can't do anything in prison."

"Are you questioning my decision, Ms. Patterson? I'd not say yes if I were you. I can still add years to your sentence." She told him that she was questioning him, that there wasn't any way for someone to spend that much time in jail. Mariam said that he was stupid. "I'll not have you slander this courtroom, young lady. You'd be better off doing what your attorney is telling you. Sit down and shut up. Would you like me to add years to your sentence?"

"Why the hell not? It's not like I'm going to live long enough to do what you've sentenced me to already." Her attorney tried to get her to sit down and shut up. "You have to be the stupidest man I've ever had dealings with. And let me tell you, I've seen a lot."

Mariam was still screaming at the judge when she was taken away. She cursed a long string of words together that he was sure she was making up. When she was out the door, silence in the courtroom sounded loudly to him. Lucas was sure that he could have heard a pin drop.

Then, as if someone had flipped a switch to turn them on, people started leaving the room and heading to the outside, where Mariam would be put in a van and taken away. Lucas held onto Micky, telling her how much he loved her.

"And I love you. How about we gather up a picnic lunch and eat it on the deck while Amber plays in the pool? I'll hold Mary Anne, and everything will be just as it should be in our home."

He thought she needed it more than she sounded like she did, and they left the courthouse. They were stopped by security as they left the room they'd been in.

"The judge, he'd like to talk to you for a moment or two. He said that he'd understand if you wanted to go home and wash the stench off of you from this. I would." The man laughed. "He's in his chambers. I'll take you there if you're willing."

"Yes, but we have a picnic to plan and go on. If he wants a lot of time, we can't do it today." The man, Washington his badge said, told him that he said it would take less than ten minutes. "All right. Do you know what this is about?"

"No, sir. I don't. But I will tell you that he didn't look all that happy when he hung up the phone and asked to see you two."

Well, that was something. Lucas had no idea what he could want, and when Micky said she was willing to listen, Lucas took her hand in his.

Lucas sat down when asked. Micky said that she'd had enough sitting for one day, and he said that he agreed. Then Moody leaned back in his chair and looked at them both. He really didn't seem like he was too thrilled with this.

"It has been asked of me to talk to you. So please, don't shoot the messenger on this. I got a call from the prison. Your mother would like to see you." Micky didn't move, not even to breathe, it looked like to him. "She has requested that you come to see her, and she promises that it has nothing to do with money or you getting her out. Ms. Mantle said that she's happy where she is."

"That's all she said, that she wants to talk to me?" Judge Moody said that it was. "May I ask how long her term is for prison? I'd like to gauge if I need to have a guard with me when or if I see her."

"Her sentencing wasn't done by me, but I can tell you, she's never getting out. She was sentenced for just over nine hundred years." Micky sat down then. "She has no chance for parole, and I'm to understand she didn't ask for something more. Usually inmates ask for a retrial if the sentence is so high. I hope your sister doesn't figure that out."

They all three laughed. Lucas had no doubt that it would have been more of a clusterfuck than the one they'd just had. Micky looked at him and he told her that he loved her.

"You'll go with me?" He said that he'd follow her to the ends of the earth. "You don't have to go that far, but I appreciate the sentiment."

Lucas cleared his throat before speaking. He knew this was just about Micky and her mother. But he wanted to make sure that she didn't come home more depressed than she had been since Beth's death.

"When we go there, if we do, what sort of setting will we be in? A room? Glass between us? I just want to make sure that I don't have to shift and hurt the population of the prison for my wife." Moody laughed again and told him it might be worth it to clear out some of the repeaters. But he told him how they'd talk to her. "All right. So, we're in a room with her with cameras going. Will there be a guard there?"

"Yes. He'll be at the ready, I've been told." Lucas knew what that meant—he'd not only have his gun out, but if there was any sort of safety, it wouldn't be on. "It's entirely up to you, Lady Manning. I can't tell you that this would be good for you, closure so to speak, but it might be just that for both of you."

"All right, I'll go. Today if that's possible." He said that it was, and he'd make the arrangements. "Thank you. I'm hoping that by the end of the day, I can happily wash my hands clean of my family."

"I do too, my lady. I do too." Judge Moody picked up his phone again and made the arrangements for them to come up today. It wasn't a far drive, but it would be stressful. Lucas decided that a limo would be better. That way he could hold her when this was done.

165

Chapter 12

Mariam knew that her daughter had been brought in. It was all over the place how she'd come in screaming so loudly about the injustice of it all that they had to put her in solitary confinement. Mariam knew that Me-Me wouldn't be in any better mood when she came out than when they put her in there. She'd come to realize that Me-Me was a dreadful person.

Not that Mariam wasn't. She knew all the things she'd done, how she'd done them. The only reason that she could come up with as to why she'd done it was because she could. Or she wanted whatever shiny thing was in front of her, no matter who it belonged to. She'd been as bad if not worse than Micky had said she was on several occasions. And now she was coming to see her.

Mariam was nervous—as well she should be, she supposed. She was going to talk to the one person in her life that she should have been proud of. Instead, because of her stupidity, she had pushed her away. Everyone really, except her other daughters—one that would do whatever dangerous thing she wanted, the other timid, but otherwise willing to join in whatever they were doing.

"Mantle, you have two visitors—your daughter and her husband. Do you want to see them?" She said that she did, and stepped up to the bars and put her hands out to be cuffed. Her ankles were done as well, and then the door was opened.

Mariam could have told them that she wasn't going to run. Nor was she going to hurt anyone. It would do her no good. Besides, it would only add on to her nine hundred and five years she was facing in here.

Shuffling down the long hall, she tried to tell herself this was going to be all right. Mariam would tell Micky what she wanted. Then she'd be put back in her cell, never to be visited again. No one, she'd figured out, would come to see a murderer and someone who dealt with drugs. She'd be alone except for the other inmates and the security staff.

As soon as she entered the room that Micky and her husband were in, she started to cry. She'd done this, put a face of hatred on her baby girl's face.

"What is it you want? If you're going to ask me to get your sentence reduced, I'm not going to do that. I'm happy where you are." She told her that she was as well. "Then what is it? I want to get home to my children and have fun."

"Children? You have children, Micky?" She told her that they were adopting a six-month old as well as a five-year-old. She didn't offer to show her photos, but Mariam wanted to be able to see them. Just this once, so she could imagine them growing up and becoming adults. Not like her. "You don't have to, but I'd like to see a picture if you have one. Just to see them."

Her husband pulled out his cell phone and then turned the picture toward her. They were beautiful. The baby looked so cuddly soft that she wanted to just touch the screen for some connection to them. One she'd never have. And the other child, with dark hair put into pigtails, looked like she'd rather be anywhere but posing for pictures. Mariam closed her eyes so that she could remember every detail about them.

"Thank you for this. I appreciate you showing them to me. I'll think about them once in a while. Not that I think they're know me or where I am, but I can dream about them and their lives with you." Mariam looked at Micky, her tears streaming down her cheeks because she had no way to wipe them away. "I'm not going to ask you for money. Nor will I beg you to forgive me. You have every right to tell me to fuck off. To never contact you again. You still might. But I wanted to thank you for taking care of Beth in her hours of need. I think that her being with you when she passed from this world to the next was the way it should have been."

"We got to know each other. Talked about our childhood, when Dad was still around. She and I connected again. And it was my pleasure to have done that for her. She never really hurt me like you two did." Mariam nodded, feeling the pain of her truthful words all the way to her heart. "If you don't want money or for me to get you out of here, what is it you want?"

"I'm going to die before I get out of here. They'll come by some morning and find that I passed in my sleep. No one will care. There won't be a person who will mourn my passing. Nary a flower will grace my coffin." Micky didn't tell her that she would mourn her; she only sat there and hated her. "I did you wrong, Micky. So many times that you cannot believe it. I killed your great grandda. I murdered him because I thought for sure that we'd all get a part of his estate. But he did the right thing, I know that now. The three of us — Beth, Me-Me, and I — would have been broke within a year."

"I'm donating what I got from the estate, minus the home, to the hospital. My family and I are going to make sure that there is enough equipment to take care of anyone that comes in." Mariam nodded. "It'll be called the Cain Mantle Wing."

"He would have gotten a kick out of that. The entire world will know that he had his name on something good." Micky held the hand of the man next to her. "I might have known your name before, but I don't remember it now."

"Lucas Manning. I'm in love with Micky. The children that we have will only be the beginning as to how many we'll take in." He kissed the back of Micky's hand, and Mariam could see that he loved her. Feel it as well. It was like a shroud covering her. It was warm and tangible. Happiness and a love that would last forever—long after she was gone, years after she was no longer a memory in her daughter's mind.

"I've asked you here for a favor. Don't think that you have to do it. I will be taken care of when I die here. There is a cemetery not far from here that holds the ghosts of ones like me. People that will never see how things progress. I'm not trying to be a martyr. I just wanted to make sure that you are really going to bury me next to Beth. I know that you have every right to tell me no. The cemetery here already has a space picked out for me should no one claim my body."

"We've already taken care of that for you and for Mariam, as I told your attorney." Mariam nodded, sobbing again that she'd not known this woman at all. "It's a lovely spot where Beth is."

When she pulled out her phone, she showed her other pictures of the children. How they were laughing and being held by them. She so wanted that. To have been around for them. Now—well, she knew that as soon as Micky and her husband left here, she'd never see her again.

"I took these pictures when the marker was set." Mariam read what it said. A loving daughter, sister, and aunt. "I know that she wasn't there for my children, but they should have known her."

"Yes, so should I have if I'd have been a better mother. Or even a better person at all." Micky nodded, agreeing with her on this. It was heartbreaking to her how much she was going to miss. Because she'd been a greedy bitch. "The spot is beautiful. It would have been a place where Beth would have sat and read a good book."

"She told me that she loved me. Told me that she was sorry more than she could tell me. My heart opened for her. Maybe because she was dying, I don't know. But we enjoyed the little time we had together. She asked me to tell you that she loved you and Mariam." Mariam asked for some tissues and was surprised when Micky got up and came to her to wipe the tears away. That, of course, made her cry all the harder. It was a kindness that she didn't deserve. "I'm not trying to hurt you with this. I'm not saying that I forgive you. I don't know if I could ever say that to you or Mariam the Second."

She smiled at the nickname Micky had given her sister. But she was no less hurt by her words, words that she deserved. Looking at Micky, she did wonder when she'd grown up, become a beautiful woman with a beautiful soul.

"You'll make sure that I'm buried next to Beth? And when her time comes, Mariam as well?" Micky said that she would. And that the prison knew as well. "I thank you for that. I fully expected that you'd say no. And I would have deserved it."

There wasn't any more to say. Mariam wanted to ask her to come back, to visit her here. But she wouldn't. It would be pressing her luck — Micky agreeing to bury her was enough. She nodded when Micky and her husband stood up. It was over.

When she was on her way back to her cell, the guard told her that her account was full. Mariam asked her what she meant.

171

"Micky Manning, she made arrangements for you to have money in your account for things you might need. A generous amount too. Did the same for your other daughter too, but she doesn't have as much." Mariam asked her how much was in each account. "You have just over a thousand. We're to let her know when it gets low again. Mariam, your daughter she's got a hundred in her account. I can understand that. Your other daughter is causing trouble already."

Another thing that she was grateful for. Micky's generosity was more than she could have hoped for. Mariam didn't need much here, but it was nice to know that she could get something if she was in need of it.

Sitting in her cell, Mariam thought of what they had talked about. How Micky had taken care of things, even before she asked. It was enough that she was going to be buried next to Beth and Mariam, but for Micky to have made it so she could get necessaries when she needed to was more than she felt she deserved.

Mariam looked at the things that had been brought to her when she'd gotten here. Sheets and a pillowcase. Two very worn towels, as well as small, sample sized shampoo, deodorant, and toothpaste. She had a toothbrush to use as well, but had to turn it in when she was finished with it. These were things that on the outside she'd taken because she needed them; now they weren't as easily had.

Lying on her bunk had become her pastime. She supposed at some point in her stay here she'd venture out. Maybe get to know people. Several jobs were available to her, and she had a month to get used to where she was and the rules, then she'd have to find some kind of employment. The growing of a vegetable garden sounded so good to her that she'd applied for that this morning.

Thinking of her grandchildren made her smile. They were so beautiful. And she'd bet well behaved as well. Micky would have them organized. Teach them the value of money and to keep their rooms clean. They'd be model children, Mariam just knew it.

When her lunch tray came, there was a fat envelope on top of it. It had been opened, as was all mail that came for the inmates, so she didn't fuss about it being done that way. Setting her tray on her bed, she dumped out the envelope. Mariam could only stare at it before she picked up the top photo with shaking hands. It was of her grandchild; all of the pictures were of her grandchildren.

Laying them out on the bed, her lunch forgotten, she looked for a note that went with them. There was one, an envelope that had also been opened. The bold handwriting on it spelled out her name. Opening it, she read what was said there.

Micky asked me to make sure that you had these. You will be getting updated pictures every few weeks. You'll never see them in person, but she wanted you to be able to see them grow up. There will not be any more conversations between you and my wife. I just wanted to make sure that you knew that. And if you don't wish to receive the pictures, then you're to tell a guard and they'll relay the message to us. Sincerely, Lord Lucas.

Never would she turn down something so dear. She went through the pictures several times before her tray was taken away. Asking the guard that came for it if there was a way for her to get tape, she wanted to hang her pictures, she told her that it was at the commissary and that she could get it there.

Mariam was so happy that she went to bed later that night with a smile. It was ironic that she had to come to prison to be happy, but she was. Closing her eyes, Mariam did something that she'd never done before. She prayed. For her family and herself.

~*~

Lucas was finished. Not just with his day, but with working too. He didn't want to leave home anymore. Staying with their children and Micky was all he wanted in life now. Thinking about their conversation with Amber, he had to chuckle a little. She was nothing if not honest with them. They'd asked her why she so readily accepted him being a dragon and the faeries that were around the house.

"Well, I didn't think you'd be killing me since you took us home. And I've seen the faeries before. Not a dragon, which is way cool, but faeries come out way early in the morning and I'd get up to see them." He told her that no one could know what she knew. "I get it. People would want to ride around on you and stuff, right?"

"Yes, that's right." He looked over her head to Micky, who was laughing. Smiling with her, he continued his talk with his little girl. "There are other people that would pay a great deal of money too, just to see one of us. And since there are six of us, a person would have to be really stupid to come and try something like that."

"Would you burn them to a crispy fry? Can we have French fries for dinner again?" He told her that he thought they were having a cookout. "Well, then can we have some tomorrow then? I really do love them."

He did as well, but he wasn't going to encourage her about things. Yesterday he'd told her how much he liked fresh tomatoes. And before he knew it, she'd gone out to get him a bag full of them. The kids at the gardens at Hudson's house were finished for the year. She'd picked what was still on the vines. There had to have been thirty tomatoes.

Cooper was coming over with Carson, and they were going

to talk about Carson leaving his job and what he could do to help the dragons out. Just so he didn't work all day, every day, as he was now. Lucas didn't blame his brother. Before Micky and the girls had come into his life, he'd enjoyed working. Now he didn't want to.

When Amber went into the house to snag a snack, Micky sat down beside him and they rocked for a little while before either of them spoke. He was enjoying the evening just as she seemed to be doing. But he could tell that she had something on her mind too.

"The prison called me. They said that they were only calling because in order to shut Mariam the Second up, they had to promise that they would call." He didn't rush her — she'd tell him in her own way. "She's upset with me, because of the little amount that is in her account. She told them to tell me that she has needs, and that since I was the only one that could get them to her, then I should just do it."

"I'm betting that went over well with you." She only smiled, and he grinned. "What did you do? I'm betting it's going to be something that I wish I'd of thought of. Did you cut her off?"

"No. I was willing to keep up with money in her account. But now instead of getting a hundred a month, she will only get fifty. Or she'll get none if she doesn't stop bothering me." She looked at him, a frown on her face. Rubbing between her eyes, Lucas asked her what else had happened. "My mother hasn't touched the money in her account since the first day. She bought some tape to hang the pictures, as well as a container of baby powder. I asked if she needed something more, thinking that she was using it for chaffing or something. And she told me that Mom was putting it on her pillow. She mentioned something about baby smell."

They rocked some more. Amber came out when Mrs.

Potter brought out Mary. They had shortened her name when Amber asked them to. She said that Mary would like having only one name. Lucas took Mary from Mrs. Potter, as it was his turn to feed her. She would gurgle and coo at them now, and happy seemed to be what she was all the time. Kissing her on the forehead when she finished her bottle and was fighting sleep, Lucas handed her to Micky. He got up to play catch with Amber.

When Cooper and Carson showed up for dinner, they had all come into the house to get Mary ready for bed and for Amber to take her bath. She liked going to her bedroom in the evening and would only come down when she was ready for sleep. It didn't bother either of them, because they knew that she was either reading or playing on her computer. Something that she'd never had before.

"I think that it's a great idea. I know that when our daughter is napping and when the boys are back in school, it'll be sort of lonely in my office. I've gotten used to the noise in the house, and without it, I don't feel right." Lucas laughed with his brother. "Did I tell you that at Carson's last checkup appointment with Clare, they told us that she was a big baby? To be honest with you, Lucas, she's so big now that I'm worried. She's only a few months old and already wearing clothing that is larger than it should be."

"She told Micky about it. Are you getting excited or nervous for when she starts to date?" Cooper told him that she wasn't going to date, ever. "I'm assuming that you've got everything ready to go. I cannot wait to see the look on your face when she makes you a grandda."

"That'll be fine, if she can make me one without having sex. Ever. And I have to tell you how impressed I am with how you and Micky are handling being parents. When we got the car seat I nearly threw it away. It took me nearly four hours to get it buckled in right. Then I had to take it out again because I had no idea that it had to face backwards. It's not easy with an infant in the house, is it?" Lucas told him that it wasn't, but it sure made a man feel good. "The boys are over the roof excited to have their little sister. I didn't know what they'd say about her, but they're just as in love with her as I am."

Dinner was just being laid out when Carson and Micky came into the dining room with them. When Carson grabbed onto the table he could see that she had her hands full trying to carry everything that a baby would need.

"I think we should go out to dinner, just you and me, Cooper." He just stood there, and Carson slapped him hard across the face. "Date. Alone. Soon."

Lucas said that he'd watch his niece, so they made the plan to have dinner tomorrow night and the boys would spend the night as well. Lucas didn't have any idea what he was getting into, but he figured that someone would do the same for him and Micky.

Dinner was, as always loud and fun. Lucas was glad that no matter what was going on in their lives, they still got together when they could. He thought his parents might have loved it more than even he did. He missed them more and more every day, it seemed like. Cooper looked over at him and spoke softly.

"I'm afraid." Micky asked him of what. "That I'll screw up her life. Perhaps be one of those parents that everyone is afraid of, and no one ever comes to the house to play."

Micky hit him and stood in front of his brother with her hand on her hip as she yelled at him. "Oh, you take the cake. Is anyone afraid of you now? No, and the children will not be either. The entire town loves you. I'm ashamed of you, Cooper Manning. What would your mother say to you right now?"

177

"She'd tell me, even though it wasn't around back then, that I should put on my big boy pants and raise her granddaughter into a wonderful person, as she knew I could." He grinned at them both. "Don't think I didn't see that you enjoyed hitting me too much. Payback is going to get you when you least expect it."

Cooper left them after hugging Micky, and they sat down as they waited for the rest of them to finish dinner. Lucas knew just what he was doing. He was waking his daughter. Cooper, he knew, would do a great job with raising this little girl.

Micky went to play with the boys after dinner. Lucas had never had something touch him so much as to see his big dragon brother holding a tiny infant. He knew that his parents would have given him a hard time as well about his fears.

On the way home, they stopped and picked up pizza for Amber as she'd been spending the evening with a new friend. She was waiting up to see pictures of the dinner that she'd missed and vowed never to miss another one. Amber was happy for the pizza. But she missed her family too. Lucas showed her the pictures that he'd taken and Micky showed hers. All in all, it had been a very eventful day.

Going to bed that night, he hugged Micky. She curled around him when he touched her, and he held her to his body. They didn't need to speak. They both knew how much they loved each other. Lucas wanted to go wake Amber and bring her and Mary to their bed to cuddle with.

"Do you suppose that we'll be able to bring more children here?" He asked her what she meant. "Well, you know, adopt more children that need us? I'd love to have a houseful of them. I kid you not, Lucas, we could have ten dozen kids and I'd be happy. With help, that is."

"Yes, help would be nice with ten dozen of them." She

pinched his arm. "I don't know why not. I mean, we have the funds for it. Hiring help would be no problem. I'd like to be involved in their childhood as much as we can."

"I'm glad to hear you say that. While I was in the nursery department this morning, I saw a little boy there that was taken from his mother. She was so high on drugs that she didn't even know where she was when she was brought in." He wondered if it was the same child he'd seen. He'd had the shakes and seemed to be very small for a newborn. "He's going to have to stay in the hospital for a few more days. But once he has the drugs out of his system and his withdrawal symptoms are gone, we can have him."

"I think I saw him there. He looked pretty tiny to me." She rolled to her back and looked at him. She asked him if he thought they shouldn't take him. "No, I didn't say that. I would love to have him here. And I'm sure that you don't mind the complications that could arise with him being a drugged baby. But it is something that we have to think about."

"With the right kind of care, I think he'll be fine. I truly believe that." Lucas kissed her on the mouth and told her that he loved her. "Then I'll tell them that we want him too."

"Micky, am I going to have to keep you from going to the hospital so much? I mean, every time you go there, if you bring home a newborn we could be buying enough diapers that we might go broke." He laughed with her. It occurred to him that she'd never asked about money. How much they had nor where it all was. It occurred to him that she didn't care. She knew that he'd take care of her.

Laughing, they got up to make arrangements for the newborn. A name would be chosen before they could bring him home too. He knew that from when they'd taken Amber and Mary. They could have changed their names then should they have wanted, but he didn't think it would be fair to them to have a different household and new names too.

Chapter 13

Wynter sat with the rest of the inmates that were at the courthouse. The pressure of all the things that had happened was weighing her down considerably, and she was sick with it. Here she was, awaiting her fate as to whether or not she was going to be murdered, or simply have to stay in prison for the rest of her life. Either one wasn't anything that she wanted. But getting anyone to help her, even to listen to her, wasn't going to help her now.

When she heard her name being called, the guard with them helped her to stand up. Wynter was shackled to ten other women, each of them scarier than the one before. Wynter nearly fell when the woman next to her jerked on the chain. When she was let loose of the chains, she shuffled her way to the front of the courtroom.

"Ms. Wynter Dawn, you are here because you killed seven people in the parking lot of the Masonry Mall. What do you have to say for yourself? Or to the families that you ruined when you had a bad day." She started to tell him that she'd done no such thing when she was jerked on again. This time she did fall. Her chain was locked to the hook in the floor, so she wasn't going anywhere. "Get up. I'm not going to tolerate you making a mockery of this courtroom."

There was a commotion out in the hallway, and she turned just as she was being helped up. The man that was standing there, with a gun in each hand, started firing as if he were trying to win a giant pink teddy bear for his girlfriend. Wynter fell to the floor this time when the chains were jerked, and looked up at the woman that had been sitting next to her. She was holding onto her own chain and Wynter's like she was waiting for them to simply snap in two. She had a very large looking handgun in the other.

"You're either dead weight or you come along with me." Wynter shook her head. "Suit yourself. I didn't want to take you anyway."

The bullet, being fired from such a close range, entered her belly before she could think about trying to fight for her life. She was suddenly jerked hard enough to make her arm snap when the man came to them with the biggest set of wire cutters she'd ever seen.

She was cut loose from the floor. Laying there, her life, she was sure, was slipping away. Wynter could hear voices screaming, also the sound of guns being fired close by. She was sure that the judge wasn't going to be too happy with this commotion either.

Wynter floated in and out of consciousness. Each time there was a different face in front of her, each of them telling her to hang on. To try and stay awake for them. One even kept telling her that they had her. Wynter's mind couldn't comprehend where she was or what she was doing. Nodding once made her sick, so she didn't do that again.

Had her for what, her mind asked herself when she was

floating again. They were going to put her in prison and toss away the key for something that she'd not done. Now she was hanging onto something that was just out of reach. Then she remembered that she'd been hurt.

"I didn't know how a gun came to be in the courtroom—I didn't have it." Wynter was pretty sure that they had laws about that sort of thing. "That judge is going to be really pissed when this is over, I think."

"Can you hear me?" Opening her eyes, it felt like lead weights were on them. The man standing there smiled, and she tried her best to smile back but nothing seemed to be working. "Are you on any kind of drugs, recreational or prescription?"

"No. I don't do that. It's expensive and dangerous." She got both her eyes open and asked him who he was. "Doctor, I didn't kill those people. Can you tell my mom that? She's all I have in the world."

"You're going to be able to tell her yourself soon enough." Nodding, she started to drift again when he said her name again. "You're going to start to feel woozy. I'm giving you something to put you under so that I can operate. All right?"

"Why bother? I think I was set to be killed by gunshot anyway." He told her that she wasn't or something like that. The medicine that he must have given her indeed made her feel woozy.

The bright lights had her cringing away from them. Wynter had no idea why she'd be seeing the sun since her cell was in the lower levels of the prison, and those were below ground. When she moved away from the light, the pain in her belly took her breath away. Then her mom was there.

"You're going to be just fine. Just fine." She'd been crying, and Wynter wanted to reach up and wipe the tears away, but she was either still cuffed to someone or she'd lost her arms.

Panicking at that thought, she asked her how much of her arm had she lost. "Nothing. You're fine. You have a broken arm — broken in three places — and you have a cast on. The other arm is being held down, so you don't pull out the IV again."

"You keep saying that." Closing her eyes, she drifted again, this time to the murders in the parking lot. While she'd not done any of the shooting, she had witnessed enough of it to know that as soon as the couple — who'd been firing at everyone that moved — found her, they were going to shoot her next.

Wynter had been coming out of the mall after doing some shopping for her mom's birthday. It was going to be great, she thought as she made her way to her car. Then she heard the first of a great many shots being fired. At first, she thought it was firecrackers. Kids were at the end of their summer vacations and blowing off steam, she thought.

She didn't know what to think when people started falling around her. Wynter felt the first sting of the four bullets she took before the body dropped on her. The man was right in her vision. He had a hole in his forehead, and his blood was dripping on her face. The weapon had been jabbing hard into her belly. Moving just enough to relieve the pressure, Wynter took the gun from him and held it in her hand just as someone started screaming close to her. She didn't move when he shouted at her not to do so. She knew then that the police had killed them while they'd been aiming at her for the final blow, she had thought.

After that she had been taken to the hospital to be treated for her wounds. No matter how many people she asked, no one would get her mom for her. Finally, after surgery that removed the bullets, she got someone to call her for her. That was when things really hit the shit fan.

During her stay at the hospital, four weeks, the police

would come in and ask her the same questions over and over daily. It got to the point that when she saw them, she'd just start answering them before they asked. They told her not to be rude—she seemed to have pissed them off somehow. Well, she'd been mad too. This was just stupid, she'd thought at the time.

"Rude? You have to come up with different questions then." The cop then took out his cuffs and cuffed her to the bed rails. "What are you doing? You can't do this to me without a good reason. Let me go."

"We have reason enough to put you in prison. Wynter Dawn, you're under arrest for being an accomplice to the murder of seven people. You have the right—"

And today she'd had to go to the courthouse to have her trial set up. She hadn't any idea what that would entail, but she'd be able to see her mom. This time without a piece of plastic between them.

Waking up again, she looked over at her mom. She was sleeping in the big chair and had a quilt that she'd made years ago wrapped around her. Mom looked exhausted. It was no wonder, Wynter thought. Her daughter had been shot—again. When her mom opened her eyes, Wynter started crying when she did.

"They're letting you come home with me for a while. But you'll have to wear one of those ankle things." Wynter asked her what had happened. "That woman that nearly killed you was trying to escape. Her boyfriend shot his way into the courtroom, and the guards there shot them both. But not before they killed three people, injuring six more, one of them you."

"Am I in trouble with that one?" Mom told her that she wasn't. And she had found a good lawyer for her. "I don't think that's going to be anything that we can afford, Mom. I don't

185

even know if we can afford a bad one with this hospital stay and the one before it. Why are people always trying to kill me?"

She'd meant it as a joke, but it failed heavily. Mom held her hand, telling her what she knew and what the papers were saying. They'd almost mentioned that they thought she might have gotten a bad deal when she'd been arrested.

"The guy that recommended this attorney, he said that the cop was having a shitty day and took it out on you. You shouldn't have been arrested, nor should he have troubled you so much. He's in trouble with his boss right now." Wynter asked her what was going to happen now. "I don't know, love. I've contacted this attorney. He sometimes takes on cases for free. Especially when he thinks an injustice has occurred. Like with you."

Wynter dozed in and out a few more times. Every time she woke, her mother was there, knitting or cutting fabric for some project. Her mom had been selling quilts since she'd been a little girl. The money had come in handy over the years too.

Waking up when it was dark outside, she saw a man sitting in the corner. She screamed, not having a clue who he was nor what he was doing in her room. When he turned on the light and smiled at her, Wynter thought that there had to be a mistake. This man was too handsome and obviously too rich for her. She pegged him for her attorney right away.

"My name is Hudson Manning. I'm going to be your attorney if you agree. Mark Haney said that you'd been arrested for no reason, and I'm going to see about getting things taken care of. All right?" She asked him where her mom was. "Ms. Dawn went down to the dining room to get herself some tea. She'll be back soon."

"I don't know why she called you. We're barely making it on our own with all this shit...stuff going on." He told her that he understood, that he was doing this pro bono. "No charge? I don't believe that. What is your angle? You going to get me in a predicament that has you charging me a bunch of money?"

"You're a distrustful little thing, aren't you? No, I'm going to work on your case, make sure that you don't have to spend any time in prison or jail. Also, I'm going to try and get you a judgment against the man who arrested you, as well as the police department. Then we'll work on your case where you were shot in the belly and got your arm broken."

She didn't believe him, and she was sure that he knew it. Wynter didn't trust many people and hadn't since she was eighteen and got caught up in some things in college. She had wanted to be an attorney herself. After the scandal was taken care of, her involvement in the scam had been washed off her record and she could continue. But then her dad had gotten sick and she'd come home.

Mr. Manning asked her a lot of questions. Most of them were about the arresting officer that day. She told him what she'd been doing and why she'd been at the mall. He asked her if she had the receipt for the purchase.

"Yes. My mom keeps stuff like that, in the event that we have to return it for some reason. But she keeps a lot of odd stuff, so that's nothing new for her." He told her that was fine, he'd get it from her. "Why are you really doing this? You lost a bet with someone? You owe some guy some money? What's the deal? And what are you?"

He just stared at her for several moments, then he smiled. Her mom came back in the room just as he was beginning to talk. But first he asked her how she knew that he wasn't human.

"Carla and David Dawn aren't my biological parents. But they couldn't have loved me any more than my real ones would have. My dad was a tiger, Mom human. You sort of get to know how shifters move when you live with one for a while." He nodded and told her that he was a dragon. "Listen buddy. If you don't want me to know, then say so. There isn't any reason for you to—"

"Wynter Snow Dawn. That's enough." Her mom could make her feel like a five-year-old with just a look. But when she used her full name, she knew that she'd really fucked up. "You'll treat this man with respect, not harp on him like a bitch. Do you understand me?"

"Yes, ma'am." Wynter looked at Mr. Manning. He was trying hard not to laugh. "You'd better let it out before you bust something. What's so funny?"

"Your name is Wynter Snow Dawn." She nodded but didn't feel inclined to tell him why. But her mother told him while she tried to think how this man was going to profit off her and her mom.

"She was literally left on our doorstep. There was a note with her, but it wasn't until later, after Wynter learned to speak French, that we knew what it said. It told us that Wynter was ours forever. That she, her mother, was on the run, and wanted her child to have a good, solid home. There were footprints in the snow to the house, but nothing that indicated that she'd left. We named her Wynter for the season that she was brought to us. Snow, because it was snowing hard enough that you couldn't see."

Wynter had heard this story a million times when she'd been younger. It never failed to make her feel like she had the best parents in the world. They could have given her up, put her in the system, but they'd taken her into their home and hearts, and she loved them too.

"That's a wonderful story, Ms. Dawn." Mom told him to call her by her first name, Carla. "All right then, if you call me

Hudson." He looked at Wynter then.

"If you can get me out of this mess, you can call me whatever you want. But not in front of my mom. She doesn't care for cursing, even though she can do it quite well when upset."

"Wynter, what a thing to say." Mom kissed her on the cheek and then held her hand. "When will you be back, Hudson?"

"Soon. I might send in one of my brothers to talk to you again. Xavier, he's good at computer work. I'm going to have him find out if the cop has done something like this before." He looked at her again. "I'd be glad to call you Wynter. I will see you in a few days."

Wynter was told that she'd be released to go home, if she agreed to wear the ankle thing and didn't try and take it off. She was so happy to get to go home that she would have agreed to have a sex change. Not that she mentioned that to them. Her mom would have bonked her on the head.

~*~

Xavier loved Wynter. She didn't cut you any slack, told you what she thought, and she would keep even someone like Carson in line. There was something so fresh and honest about her that he was very disappointed that she'd not been his mate. Now he had to hope that she was Tristan's. She'd have him in knots in seconds.

"I have his name here, his record, as well as some hidden things that were on his computer. He's not a nice guy." Wynter asked him what he'd found, and if she was going to jail with Xavier when he got his ass caught. "No, neither of us will go to jail for this. First of all, no one will ever know that I was in his file, and secondly, I'm that good."

She snorted at him. "No one is that good. You can bet that if I'm involved in something, I'm going to get caught. Trouble just seems to follow me around like a shadow on a sunny day." He

189

laughed. "You're nothing like your brother, are you? I mean, he's all tense and shit. Not Hudson, but the other guy, Lincoln."

"Lincoln is a thinker, and sometimes people think that he's not listening to them. It's because he's thinking of and discarding scenarios that he could get into. Have any of my other brothers come to see you yet?" She told him no and asked him how many there were of them. "Six of us. We're all dragons. I'm to understand that you don't believe us."

"It's not that. Okay, it is that, but what you don't understand is, I have a tattoo on my left leg that's a dragon. I have no idea where it came from. Mom said it was there when they found me." Xavier stiffened. As calmly as he could, he asked to see it. "Sure. But I have to tell you, it's changed in the last few hours. It's itchy for one thing, and now it's in color."

"Itchy? Like a burning itchy, or something more?" She told him that she didn't understand. "Is it itchy, or simply a burning that you're trying to soothe?"

"Oh, let me think." While she seemed to be concentrating on what he'd asked her, she pulled up the gown she had on. The tattoo was from her ankle to her thigh. Holding onto the bed, she told him that it was burning, not itching.

"You said that it became in color. When did that part start?" She asked him if he was freaking out. "Yes. Yes, I am. You have the mark of a dragon. I would imagine that your parents were dragons. But as to why you have the mark or why it's suddenly in color, I have no idea. I have to talk to my sister-in-law about this. She'll know. Then if not her, then my brother, Cooper. May I take a picture of it?"

"Yeah, sure. But you're starting to scare me too. What the hell do you mean, I could be a dragon? I would think by now, I'd have been able to figure that out, don't you?" He said that he didn't know and would really try and get her some answers.

190

"I hope so. I've tried to have this removed several times, but it comes back. The older I got, the bigger it got too."

The dragon looked like Tristan's — in fact, one could almost say that it was the twin to his. It was his shade of blue. Even the dragon's eyes were the same color as his brother's.

He took pictures of it. The way that it wrapped around her ankle all the way up to her thigh. The head of the monster sized dragon was in warrior stage, the only part of him that was. But he couldn't see under it, so he assumed that part. The dragon's claws looked if he was digging into skin so that he could hang on. Everything about this dragon scared the shit out of him.

Xavier nearly screamed when Cooper got back to him. *You say that it's huge. I can't tell the size that her leg is. I mean, is she tall, leggy?* He told him both. She had beautiful legs. *Do me a favor. Have someone put their hand just over the head. That should give me some reference.*

Wynter willingly did as he asked. Taking a picture of it again, Xavier sent it on to Cooper. He had no idea why he needed to know how big it was, but Cooper would know more than most. Xavier went over the case history while he waited. A good twenty or so minutes later Cooper asked another favor for him.

I want you, and only you, to put your hand over the dragon's head. Don't touch it — that could be dangerous. If it does what I think it'll do, then I know what it is. He put his hand over the head, about two feet from it. Realizing that he didn't know how close, he asked Cooper. *It says inches. Christ, Xavier, this is scary huge.*

Xavier decided not to tell Wynter what Cooper said. Both of them were fucking freaked out as it was. Xavier realized that his hand was trembling. And so was Wynter. When she put her hand over his while still about a foot away, he seemed to calm a little.

"Whatever happens, we'll have the mystery of the dragon. You just do what your brother told you, and I'll try my best not to get all girly on you and scream." He smiled. Xavier already loved this woman. She was just what his brother needed. If she was indeed Tristan's mate.

None of them knew what to expect. When his hand was only about five inches from her leg, he did act all girly and Wynter fainted. Christ almighty, the thing came up to touch his hand.

Wynter wasn't out long, just long enough for him to sit on the floor with his head between his legs. He could hear Cooper yelling at him. But at this moment, he needed to just absorb. A sigil, he'd already figured out, had touched him. Telling Cooper to wait, he sat there until he felt calm again. Xavier looked up at Wynter.

"Are you okay?" She just stared at him. "I've never seen anything like that before. It touched me."

"Am I fucking okay? That's what you ask me when you've just petted a fucking dragon that was on my skin? Hell no, I'm not okay. I have a living thing on my fucking leg." Her mom didn't even hush her when she cursed. She looked a little pale as well. "Mom, why don't you sit down? I don't want you to pass out too."

"I'm not sure what to think or to do. Yes, I'll sit." She did, then stood up again. "I can't sit—I just saw a dragon rise up from your leg."

Xavier could finally talk to his brother. *I did what you wanted. And the next time you know something like this might happen, fucking tell me. You had plenty of time to say, hey Xavier, here's the thing. I think that dragon will want you to touch him. A couple of sentences and I'd have been prepared. As it was, I screamed then nearly passed out from it. Christ, Cooper, the dragon lifted up off her skin into my*

192

hand. It even purred a little.

To be honest with you, the book I'm reading from only says to have a dragon touch the dragon. I guess when Sadie was drawing the picture, she thought that that would clear it up for us. He said that it didn't. Xavier stood up and asked Wynter if it had hurt. She was still shaken but told him she'd not felt a thing. Cooper told him the rest. *She's the daughter of two dragons. Dragons, Xavier, like us. Someone changed her so that she'd be able to shift from dragon to woman like they did us. I'm assuming it was Sadie, but I have no way of telling now. Ask her about her parents, the real ones.*

Sadie was the powerful witch that had helped their dad with changing them so that they'd be human. Unlike most shifters, they were their other halves, then turned into humans. This woman was as well, but it stumped him as to why she had a sigil of one on her skin.

Xavier told Cooper what had happened when she'd been left out in the cold. Cooper wanted him to touch the dragon again but didn't want him to press his luck. There was a good possibility that he could pull it from her body, and that would be the end of things here.

What do we do now? We can't leave her here. Someone will say something about the dragon, and that will make her a target of some very unscrupulous men. Cooper agreed. *But how do we get her there? And I tell you, Cooper, this dragon is the twin of Tristan. I have an idea that she'll be his mate.*

I saw that as well. I won't say anything to him until we find out for sure. And Winnie is on her way there. Winnie suddenly popped into the room. He didn't have any time to prepare Wynter and her mom for her arrival. *Winnie is going to bring Wynter. You bring her mom. That way, it won't look as if you're kidnapping her.*

That's all I need. Xavier explained what was going to happen. Wynter asked several questions, just as he figured she would.

193

"You'll go to Cooper's house. He will have a better handle on this than I do. Your mom and I, we'll travel by car, so you can expect us in about an hour or so."

"You know what this is, and it's bad, isn't it?" He told her that he could see nothing bad with the dragon, but now that it had changed, they needed to take precautions. Like not letting anyone else see it. "All right. But if you so much as touch my mom with intent, I will do what I can to hunt you down."

"I would never harm either of you. On this you have my word." Xavier was thinking about what he had to do and looked at Winnie. "They have to see her in here after we've gone. That way no one can say, not even remotely, that we took her."

"That's a good one. All right. You two leave, and I'll have her call for something for pain." Wynter told Winnie that she was right here. "Yes, you are. But we're better at hiding ourselves and taking care than you are. Trust us."

He and Carla left the room. Xavier made a show of letting the people at the desk know that they were leaving. Putting a business card on the desktop, Xavier explained that he was Wynter's attorney and that he'd like to be called if anything happened. He hoped this would work. Getting in his car, it was all he could do to remain calm while he started it. Xavier felt like a drowning man and was terrified. Not for himself, but for the younger woman. But they'd protect her even if she wasn't Tristan's mate. She was special.

Before You Go...

HELP AN AUTHOR

write a review

THANK YOU!

Share your voice and help guide other readers to these wonderful books. Even if it's only a line or two your reviews help readers discover the author's books so they can continue creating stories that you'll love. Login to your favorite retailer and leave a review. Thank you.

AWARD WINNING, BESTSELLING AUTHOR

Kathi Barton, winner of the Pinnacle Book Achievement award as well as a best-selling author on Amazon and All Romance books, lives in Nashport, Ohio with her husband Paul. When not creating new worlds and romance, Kathi and her husband enjoy camping and going to auctions. She can also be seen at county fairs with her husband who is an artist and potter.

Her muse, a cross between Jimmy Stewart and Hugh Jackman, brings her stories to life for her readers in a way that has them coming back time and again for more. Her favorite genre is paranormal romance with a great deal of spice. You can visit Kathi online and drop her an email if you'd like. She loves hearing from her fans. aaronskiss@gmail.com.

Follow Kathi on her blog: http://kathisbartonauthor.blogspot.com/